ILLUSTRATED CLASSICS

The Three Musketeers

Alexandre Dumas

Adapted by
Bookmatrix Ltd

Edited by
Claire Black

Published by

Berryland
Books
www.berrylandbooks.com

The Three Musketeers

Alexandre Dumas

First Published in 2006 • Copyright © Berryland Books 2006
ISBN 1-84577-095-1 • Printed in India

Contents

CHAPTER 1

D'Artagnan

On the first Monday of April 1625, the market town of Meung, France was in a state of chaos. Many citizens, stopping their work, rushed towards the Jolly Miller inn, where a noisy group had gathered and was increasing every minute.

Those were the times when there was a lot of turbulence in the State. The nobles made war against each other; the King against the dinal; and

Spain, against the King. In addition, there were the robbers and rogues, who made war upon everybody. The citizens always took up arms readily against the thieves or rogues, often against nobles, sometimes against the King, but never against the Cardinal or Spain.

It was due to this habit that on hearing all the clamour, curious citizens rushed towards the market street and gathered before the Jolly Miller inn. Once there, the cause of the hubbub was evident to all.

It was a young man - dressed in a woollen close fitting jacket of faded blue colour and a kind of feather cap. He had a long brown face, high cheekbones, open and intelligent eyes, and a hooked, but finely chiselled nose.

However, it was the pony the young man rode, that was the object of widespread curiosity. The pony was about fourteen years old. Its hide was of a yellow colour, and there was absolutely no hair in its tail. And above all this, the pony had a peculiarly strange gait. At a time when everybody was a connoisseur of horses, the appearance of this pony caused an unfavourable feeling.

This feeling was painfully perceived by its owner, young D'Artagnan of Gascony. He was on his way to Paris, to join the King of France's Musketeers.

Before his departure, his father had said, "I have nothing to give you, my son, but fifteen crowns, my horse, and some advice. Remember, always remain worthy of your name of a gentleman, which has been worthily borne by your ancestors for five hundred years. You must be brave for two reasons: the first, you are a Gascon; and the second, you are my son. I have taught you how to handle a sword; never fear fights, but seek adventures."

And so, endowed with three gifts from his father - the yellow horse, fifteen crowns, and a letter for M. de Tréville, (who was previously his father's neighbour) - D'Artagnan made his way towards Paris. Despite all the curious glances and suppressed smiles his horse generated, he rode his pony proudly and majestically till he reached the city of Meung, where he or rather his pony became the object of universal curiosity.

As D'Artagnan was climbing down from his pony at the gate of the Jolly Miller inn, he overheard a gentleman making fun of his pony, while his two companions burst into fits of laughter.

D'Artagnan felt extremely insulted. He walked up to the men and said in an angry tone, "What are you laughing at, gentlemen? Tell me and we will laugh together!"

The stranger looked at him with a slight smile and, turning towards his two comrades, resumed ridiculing the horse.

D'Artagnan became furious. "There are people who laugh at the horse, but would not dare to laugh at the master," he cried.

"I laugh when I please, sir," said the stranger, and turned towards the inn. But, D'Artagnan was not a person to allow a man who had ridiculed him, to escape. He drew out his sword crying, "Turn, or I will strike you from behind!"

The stranger turned and drew his sword; but at the same moment, his two companions, accompanied by the host of the inn, fell upon D'Artagnan with sticks, shovels, and tongs.

The unequal fight went on for a little while. At last, D'Artagnan received a heavy blow on his forehead and fainted.

The host, fearing unpleasant consequences, took him upstairs to his wife's room. She dressed his wounds, and covered his head with bandages.

Meanwhile, the host went to the gentleman to check he wasn't hurt. The host went on to inform him that a letter had been found on the person of the young man. "It is a letter addressed to 'Monsieur de Tréville, captain of the Musketeers,'" he announced.

The effect this news had on the gentleman

was profound.

"What! Has this youth been sent by Tréville? And why?" he murmured.

"His things and his bag are with him?" he asked the host. "Has he taken off his doublet?"

"On the contrary, everything is in the kitchen," replied the host.

Then, the gentleman asked the host to have his horses saddled for his departure.

"Milady will soon pass by and I don't want her to be seen by this fellow. I had better get on horseback, and go and meet her," he murmured to himself.

In the meantime, D'Artagnan was feeling much better and was able to move, so he went down to the kitchen. There, through the window he saw the same gentleman he had fought with that morning, talking to a beautiful woman in a carriage. The lady was around twenty to twenty-two years of age and was pale and fair, with long curls falling over her shoulders.

D'Artagnan tried to listen to their conversation. He heard the lady say, "…so my orders are…"

"Yes, return immediately to England and inform him if the Duke of Buckingham leaves London, while I shall return to Paris," the gentleman replied.

"What!" cried the woman, "Without punishing this insolent boy?"

At that moment, D'Artagnan, who had heard

everything, rushed forward through the open door and cried, "This insolent boy punishes others! I hope you will not escape me this time."

On seeing D'Artagnan, the man bowed to the lady and quickly sprang into his saddle. At the same time, the lady's coachman applied his whip vigorously to his horses. Both of them set out in two opposite directions.

"Coward!" cried D'Artagnan. But he could not manage to run more than a few steps because of his wounds, and fell down in a faint.

D'Artagnan, with the help of an ointment his mother had given him, was almost cured in two days. But, when the time came to pay the host, he found that the letter addressed to M. de Tréville had disappeared from his pocket!

"My letter of recommendation!" cried D'Artagnan "Where is my letter?" And he flew into a tremendous rage.

"Was that letter very valuable?" asked the frightened host, who had rushed in, hearing his cry.

"It contained my fortune!" said D'Artagnan. "I will complain to Monsieur de Tréville, and Monsieur de Tréville will complain to the King."

"That letter is not lost! It has been stolen from you," cried the host, almost panicky by now, "stolen by the gentleman who was here yesterday. I saw him come down into the kitchen. He was looking around for something." "Then that's my thief," replied D'Artagnan.

D'Artagnan paid the host for the food and lodging, remounted his yellow horse, and left on his journey with a troubled mind. He reached Paris, without any further incidents.

There, he sold his horse for three crowns and proceeded towards De Tréville's headquarters on foot.

CHAPTER 2

Meeting the Captain of the Musketeers

M. de Tréville was a friend of King Louis XIII. The King had made him the captain of his Musketeers – his courageous soldiers and Guards. The King's Musketeers were the bravest of all.

When D'Artagnan visited M. de Tréville's place, he saw the Musketeers standing in small groups, duelling, cracking jokes and enjoying their drinks. After D'Artagnan had stood for a while in this crowd, a person came to him and asked him whom he wanted to meet. After he had narrated his business, D'Artagnan was led into M. de Tréville office.

The captain of the Musketeers was in a very bad mood. Nevertheless, he politely greeted the young man and requested him to wait till he finished with others. He then stuck his head out of the door, and called out loudly, "Athos! Porthos! Aramis!"

Two Musketeers answered to these names. When the two had entered and the door was closed behind them, M. de Tréville turned towards them angrily.

"Do you know what the King said to me?" cried he. "He told me that he should from now on employ his Musketeers from among the Guards of the Cardinal."

"The Guards of the Cardinal!" cried the Musketeer with a great height, who was called Porthos. "Why so?"

"Yes, yes," continued M. de Tréville, "and his Majesty was right. The Cardinal told me that the day before yesterday a few drunken Musketeers got into a fight with the Cardinal's Guards. And you three were among them! Don't deny it, you were recognized; you Porthos, Aramis, and…I don't see Athos! Where is he?"

"Sir," replied Aramis, sadly, "he is ill, very ill!"

"Ill! Wounded is more like it!" cried M. de Tréville. "I will not have my Musketeers quarrelling in the streets. The Cardinal's Guards will never put themselves in a position to be arrested. And I am sure they would prefer dying to being arrested or escaping."

"Well, captain," said Porthos, "the truth is that though we were six against six, but we were not captured by fair means. Before we had time to draw our swords, two of our party were dead, while Athos was grievously wounded. But we did not surrender! They dragged us away by force."

"And I assure you that I killed one of them

with his own sword, for mine was broken," said Aramis.

"I did not know that," replied M. de Tréville, in a rather softened tone. "The Cardinal exaggerated, I believe."

At that very moment, the tapestry was raised and a noble and handsome face appeared at the door, looking very pale.

"Athos!" cried the two Musketeers.

"Athos!" cried M. de Tréville.

"You called me, sir," said Athos to captain Tréville, in a weak but firm voice.

M. de Tréville was touched to the bottom of his heart by the courage shown by the injured Athos. He rushed towards him and said, "I was about to say to these gentlemen that I forbid my Musketeers to expose their lives needlessly. The King knows how brave you are and would not like you to waste your lives."

A loud murmur of satisfaction hailed the last words of the captain. Athos, who had until now held back his pain, was at this point overcome by it and fell down in a faint. Immediately, at a sign from M. de Tréville, Porthos and Aramis carried off their comrade in their arms.

When they had left, M. de Tréville realised the presence of the young man he had asked to wait.

"Pardon me, for having kept you waiting," he said with a smile. "What can I do for my friend's son?"

"Sir," said D'Artagnan, "I had thought of requesting you to take me as a Musketeer. But now I have realised the value of such a favour, and I am afraid that I am not worth it."

"Well, young man," replied M. de Tréville, "no one can become a Musketeer unless he performs some act of great courage or serves in the lower regiment for two years; and his Majesty's decision is always necessary."

"Oh sir, only I know how much I miss the letter of introduction which my father gave me,"

said D'Artagnan, sadly. "But it was stolen from me."

He then related the adventure at Meung, and described the unknown gentleman in detail.

"Tell me," asked Tréville, "did this gentleman have a slight scar on his cheek?"

"Yes! On his right cheek! How do you know that? Do you know who this man is?"

"And you say that he was waiting for a lady and left immediately after talking to her for a minute. Was she an Englishwoman? Did you hear her name?"

"He called her Milady."

"It is he! It must be he!" murmured Tréville. "I thought he was still at Brussels!"

"Sir, if you know who this man is," cried D'Artagnan, "tell me his name, for I wish to avenge myself."

"Be careful, young man," said M. de Tréville, "do not pick up any fight with him. Forget the entire episode and leave the idea of revenge."

Then M. de Tréville sat down in order to write a letter of recommendation to the academy for D'Artagnan's training, so that he would be able to join the King's Musketeers after his training.

Meanwhile, D'Artagnan went up to the window and looked out. Suddenly, he rushed out of the room, crying, "He shall not escape me this time."

"Who, who?" asked M. de Tréville.

"My thief!" replied D'Artagnan and disappeared.

CHAPTER 3

Athos, Porthos, and Aramis

D'Artagnan crossed the entrance hall in three bounds and ran into Athos who was coming out of one of M. de Tréville's private rooms, hitting his shoulder violently. Athos, whose shoulder was already injured, uttered a cry of pain.

"Excuse me," said D'Artagnan, "I am sorry I hurt you, but I am in a hurry."

"Sir," said Athos, letting him go, "you are very

impolite; I understand that you are not from Paris." D'Artagnan had already gone down three or four stairs when Athos' remark made him stop.

"Sir, even if I have come from far, you are no one to give me a lesson in good manners, I warn you," he said.

"Then perhaps I should give you a lesson in duel!" said Athos.

And the two decided to meet near the Carmes-Deschaux about noon.

D'Artagnan set off running, hoping that the stranger had not gone very far. At the street gate, he saw Porthos talking with the soldier on guard, and between the two there was just enough room for a man to pass.

D'Artagnan thought it was sufficient for him. As he was about to pass, the wind blew out Porthos' long cloak, and D'Artagnan ran straight into the middle of it.

D'Artagnan was trying to come out of the folds of the cloak, when Porthos cried, "Good

Lord! You must be mad to run against people in this manner."

"Excuse me," said D'Artagnan, "but I am in a hurry as I am running after someone, and…".

"And do you always forget your eyes when you happen to be in a hurry? I warn you that you shall be punished if you run against Musketeers in this fashion," said Porthos.

"Punished!" cried D'Artagnan. "And who is going to punish me?" he laughed.

Porthos became tremendously angry upon this, and challenged D'Artagnan to a duel near Carmes-Deschaux at one o'clock.

D'Artagnan agreed, and proceeded on his chase. But, by then he had lost track of the man he was running after. D'Artagnan looked around for some time and finally gave up the chase.

As he was thinking about the events of the whole day, he arrived near Treville's place once again. There, he saw Aramis chatting casually with three gentlemen of the King's Guards in front

of that hotel. Then he noticed that Aramis had dropped his handkerchief, and stepped upon it. Wishing to be of some help, D'Artagnan rushed towards him. Then, bending down, he pulled the handkerchief from under Aramis' foot, in spite of all the efforts Aramis made to detain it.

"I believe, sir, that this is your handkerchief," D'Artagnan said, holding it out to Aramis.

The handkerchief was richly embroidered,

and perfumed. Aramis was very embarrassed and he snatched the handkerchief from D'Artagnan's hand.

"Ah, ah, Aramis!" cried one of the Guards, "will you continue denying that you are on good terms with Madame de Bois-Tracy, who has kindly lent you one of her handkerchiefs?"

The King's Guards burst into a loud laugh.

D'Artagnan realised that he had embarrassed Aramis and that he should offer an apology. So, D'Artagnan went up to Aramis with a good feeling and said, "Sir, you will excuse me, I hope."

"I suppose that you are not a fool sir, and you know very well that people do not step on pocket handkerchiefs without a reason," said Aramis.

"Monsieur, you act wrongly in trying to humiliate me so," said D'Artagnan.

"Why did you give me the handkerchief then?" asked Aramis.

"Why did you let it fall?" asked D'Artagnan.

"I have said, sir that the handkerchief did not

fall from my pocket."

"And by saying so you have lied twice, sir, as I saw it fall."

"Oh, I think there's only one way to teach you how to behave yourself," cried Aramis. "Meet me at two o'clock at the hotel of M. de Tréville. There, I will point out to you the best place and time for a duel."

The two men bowed and separated, and D'Artagnan went on the road to the Carmes-Deschaux as it was about to be noon. As he went, he murmured to himself, "Definitely I can't draw back now; but, if I am killed, at least I shall be killed by a Musketeer!"

CHAPTER 4

King's Musketeers vs. Cardinal's Guards

At exactly twelve o' clock, D'Artagnan reached the scheduled place and found Athos who, still suffering grievously from his wound, was seated on a stone waiting for him. The two adversaries greeted each other.

"Sir," said Athos, "I have engaged two of my friends as seconds."

"I have no seconds, Monsieur, as I have arrived

just today morning," said D'Artagnan. "But I am honoured to cross swords with someone who has agreed to fight with me in spite of having a painful wound."

"Very painful, and it hurts like devil," said Athos.

"If you'd permit me, I have a miraculous balm for wounds - given to me by my mother, and I am sure it will cure your wound within three days."

D'Artagnan spoke these words with a simplicity that emphasised his courtesy, without throwing any doubt upon his courage. Athos acknowledged his proposal with a gracious nod and said, "You are a man of heart, Monsieur. I have a feeling that if we don't kill each other in this duel, we shall become good friends. Ah, here come my friends."

D'Artagnan turned in the direction pointed to by Athos, and saw Aramis and Porthos approaching.

"What!" he cried with astonishment, "are your

seconds M. Aramis and M. Porthos?"

"Certainly! Don't you know that we are never seen without each other, and that we are called as the Three Inseparables?"

In the meantime, Porthos had come up, waved his hand to Athos, and then turning towards D'Artagnan, stopped, astonished.

"Ah, ah!" said Porthos, "what does this mean?"

"This is the gentleman I am going to fight with," said Athos.

"Why, I am also going to fight with him," said Porthos.

"Well, and I too," said Aramis, coming up in his turn.

"Well then, let's begin right away," said D'Artagnan.

It was quarter past twelve and the sun was at its peak, when the duel began. However, the two swords had hardly clashed when a group of Cardinal's Guards turned towards the convent of

Carmes-Deschaux.

"The Cardinal's Guards!" cried Aramis and Porthos at the same time. "Keep your swords down gentlemen!"

But it was too late; the Cardinal's Guards had already seen everything. They came up and ordered their arrest, citing the Cardinal's decree against duelling.

"There are five of them," whispered Athos, "and we are three. We shall lose again. But I would prefer to die on the spot than again appear before captain Tréville as a conquered man."

Meanwhile, D'Artagnan had made his decision. He turned towards Athos and his friends, and said, "Gentlemen, you said you are three, but I think we are four."

"But you are not one of us," said Porthos.

"It's true that I do not wear the uniform, but I am in spirit and heart a Musketeer," replied D'Artagnan.

"Well, you are a real good fellow," said Athos.

holding the young man's hand. "What is your name, my brave fellow?"

"D'Artagnan, sir."

"Well, then, Athos, Porthos, Aramis, and D'Artagnan, forward!" cried Athos.

And the nine warriors rushed at one another. D'Artagnan, despite a lack of practice, fought with passion and dexterity.

Within a short time, D'Artagnan and the

Musketeers had wounded four soldiers, killed a fifth one, and were on their way back to the hotel of M. de Tréville.

The four men walked arm in arm, occupying the whole street, and greeting every Musketeer they met. D'Artagnan's heart throbbed with wild joy as he walked down between Athos and Porthos.

"Though I am not a Musketeer yet," he said to his new friends, "at least I have entered upon my apprenticeship, haven't I?"

When M. de Tréville heard of the fight with the Cardinal's men, he scolded his Musketeers in public and congratulated them in private. Then he went to see the King.

But he was too late; the King had already been informed about the incident by the Cardinal.

Finally, when M. De Treville met King Louis in the evening, the King said, "Well, Monsieur, you say it is his Eminence's Guards who sought a quarrel with your Musketeers?"

"Yes sir, as they always do," replied the captain.

And he went on to relate the fight in detail, mentioning how bravely young D'Artagnan had fought and wounded the leader of the Guards, Jussac.

"That young boy wounded Jussac!" exclaimed the King, "Jussac is one of the finest swordsmen in the kingdom!"

"Well then it is a victory!" continued the King, glowing with pleasure, "a complete victory! Bring me all four together; I wish to thank them all at once."

M. de Tréville asked the four men to join them.

"Come in, my braves," said the King, "come in; I have a scolding for you."

He then took a handful of gold and put it into the hand of D'Artagnan.

"Here," he said, "is a proof of my satisfaction."

D'Artagnan put the forty pistoles into his pocket and thanked his Majesty most heartily.

After the Musketeers had left, the King said in a low voice, "Well, captain, as you have no room in the Musketeers, place this young man in the company of the Guards of Monsieur Des Essarts, your brother-in-law. Ah, Tréville! I can well imagine the face the Cardinal will make! He will be furious; but I don't care. I am doing what is right."

When Tréville left the King and rejoined the Musketeers, he found them sharing the forty pistoles with D'Artagnan.

CHAPTER 5

Beginning of a War

D'Artagnan asked his three new friends as to how he should spend his share of the money. Athos advised him to order a good meal, Porthos asked him to engage a lackey—a servant who can take care of his needs and Aramis told him to look for a place to stay.

All three jobs were completed that very day,

and D'Artagnan hired a lackey called Planchet.

Athos' lackey was called Grimaud. Although Athos was barely thirty years old and was intelligent and extremely handsome, his reserve, roughness and silence made almost an old man of him. Grimaud, too, was as quiet as his master. They almost never spoke to one another.

Porthos had a character exactly opposite to that of Athos. He not only talked much, but he talked loudly, little caring whether anybody listened to him or not. His lackey Mousqueton was also loud and rough.

Aramis was the most reserved of the three, and his lackey, Bazin was a pious fellow who looked forward to Aramis' entering the priesthood.

Soon, the three Musketeers became very attached to young D'Artagnan. They met three or four times a day, whether for duels, business, or pleasure.

Meanwhile, the forty pistoles of King Louis XIII had all been used up and the four friends had become quite penniless. One day as they were desperately trying to find some way to earn money, D'Artagnan received an unusual visitor.

"I have heard of you being spoken of as a very brave young man," said the visitor. "This made me decide to confide to you a secret."

"Speak, Monsieur," said D'Artagnan.

"I have a wife whose name is Constance Bonacieux. She is a seamstress to the Queen. Yesterday morning she was carried off, as she was coming out of her workroom."

"But why was your wife carried off?"

"I believe that my wife has been carried off because of the secret love affair of a much greater lady."

"Of the Q…" D'Artagnan checked himself.

"Yes, sir," replied the terrified man, in a tone so low that he was scarcely audible.

"And with whom?"

"With the Duke of…Duke of Buckingham!"

"The Duke of Buckingham - the Prime Minister

of England!" cried D'Artagnan. "Ah! It begins to grow clear."

"You see, the marriage of King Louis of France, and Anne of Austria was arranged simply to keep peace between France and Spain. But now that Spain is an enemy of France, the Queen is still loyal to her native State. This fact is particularly disliked by the Cardinal. Moreover, there is her affair with the Duke… Now the Queen believes that some one has written to the Duke of Buckingham in her name, to make him come to Paris; to draw him into some trap."

"But what has your wife to do with all this?"

"Her loyalty to the Queen is known, and so they wish either to remove her from her mistress, or to threaten her. They want to obtain her Majesty's secrets, and make use of my wife as a spy."

"That is very probable," said D'Artagnan; "but do you know the man who carried her off?"

"I can describe his appearance. He is a noble

of arrogant behaviour, black hair, piercing eye, and a scar on his temple."

"A scar on his temple!" cried D'Artagnan; "and a piercing eye. Why, that's my man of Meung! Now with one blow I shall obtain two revenges. Are you sure of the description?"

"As sure as my name is Bonacieux…"

"I think I have heard your name before."

"It is possible, sir, as I am your landlord. You must be busy in your important occupations as, you have forgotten to pay me my rent since you have come."

"I am sorry for such conduct, believe me. If I can be of any service to you…" replied D'Artagnan.

"I just want to have my wife back safely. And you are the only one who can help me find her," the landlord replied.

D'Artagnan promised to help his landlord and assured him the safe return of his wife. When Athos, Porthos and Aramis returned D'Artagnan told his friends all that had passed between him and his landlord, and how the man had carried off the landlord's wife.

While the four were talking, a sudden noise of footsteps was heard upon the stairs. Then, the door was thrown violently open, and the landlord rushed into the room.

"Save me, gentlemen, save me!" cried he. "Four men have come to arrest me! Please, save me!"

Porthos and Aramis arose. "One moment," cried D'Artagnan, making a sign to his friends to replace their half-drawn swords. "One moment, we need to act wisely."

At this moment, four soldiers of the Cardinal's Guards appeared at the entrance. But when they saw the four Musketeers standing with swords at their sides, they hesitated to advance further.

"Come in, gentlemen, come in," said D'Artagnan. "We are all faithful servants of the King and the Cardinal."

"Then, gentlemen, you have no objection to

our carrying out our orders?" asked a guard.

"Not at all," replied D'Artagnan.

"But you promised me…" whispered the poor trader.

"We can save you only if we ourselves are free," replied D'Artagnan in a low and hurried tone; "and if we try to defend you, they will arrest us too."

"Now, gentlemen, come, take away this man!" said D'Artagnan.

The officers were full of thanks, and took away their victim.

"And now, gentlemen," said D'Artagnan, "all for one, one for all; that is our motto, is it not?"

"All for one, one for all!" cried the Musketeers.

And from that moment on, they were at war with the Cardinal.

CHAPTER 6

An Evil Plot

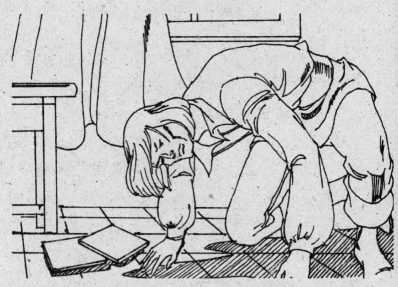

The apartment of M. Bonacieux became a mouse-trap; meaning, whosoever came there was placed under suspicion and arrested by the Cardinal's men. D'Artagnan did not stir from his apartment and observed everybody from his windows; he saw all who came and were trapped. He had removed some of the tiles of his floor and he heard all that passed between the inquisitors and the accused.

The day after Bonacieux's arrest, at nine in the evening, D'Artagnan heard a knock at the street door. The door was opened instantly and shut: someone had been caught in the mouse-trap!

D'Artagnan flew to his peep-hole, and laid himself down on the floor at full length to listen. He heard the cries of a woman. She was crying and screaming.

"But I am the mistress of the house, gentlemen! I tell you I am Madame Bonacieux!" cried the unfortunate woman.

"Madame Bonacieux!" murmured D'Artagnan. "Have I found her?"

"You are the one we were waiting for," cried the questioners.

"They are gagging her, they are going to drag her away," cried D'Artagnan to himself, springing from the floor. "Planchet, Planchet!"

"Sir."

"Quick, run and get Athos, Porthos, and Aramis.

Tell them to arm themselves and come here. Ah, I remember; Athos is at M. de Tréville's."

"Oh, Monsieur!" cried Planchet. "You will kill yourself."

"Keep quiet," cried D'Artagnan, and he jumped nimbly down onto the floor below. Then he went straight to the door, and knocked.

As the door opened, D'Artagnan rushed into M. Bonacieux's apartment with his sword in hand. The spring-door closed.

Next, M. Bonacieux's neighbours heard loud cries, clashing of swords, and breaking of furniture, and rushed to their window to see what had happened. They saw four frightened men run out of M. Bonacieux's room, leaving behind patches of their clothes and fragments of their cloaks.

Meanwhile, D'Artagnan turned towards Madame Bonacieux. The poor woman had fallen back upon an armchair in a half-faint. However, she soon recovered her senses and held out her hands to D'Artagnan with a smile.

"Ah, sir!" said she, "You have saved me. Allow me to thank you." D'Artagnan saw that Constance Bonacieux was a young and beautiful woman, and had the sweetest smile in the world. To him, she seemed too young to be the wife of the old landlord.

"Madame," said he, "I have only done what every gentleman would have done in my place. You owe me no thanks."

"What did these men want from me, and why is M. Bonacieux not here?" asked the woman.

"Madame, they are the agents of the Cardinal; and your husband, M. Bonacieux, was taken away to the Bastille yesterday evening."

"Oh, my God!" cried Madame Bonacieux.

"Madame, how did you escape?"

"I took advantage of a moment when they left me alone; I let myself down from the window with the help of my sheets and escaped."

"Now let us get away from this house, first," said D'Artagnan.

D'Artagnan left Madame Bonacieux safely at the Louvre - the royal palace, and went back to his house. On his way back, D'Artagnan kept thinking of Madame Bonacieux. He had fallen in love with the young and charming Constance.

D'Artagnan went to M. de Tréville's to tell him about all the events that had taken place, but he was not in his hotel.

On his way back from the hotel, D'Artagnan

saw two people whose appearance struck his attention. One was a man, the other a woman. The woman had Madame Bonacieux's figure and wore a hood that covered her face, while the man wore the uniform of the Musketeers and held his handkerchief up to his face.

Curious, D'Artagnan followed them.

He had hardly gone twenty steps before he became convinced that the woman was really Madame Bonacieux. D'Artagnan grew jealous.

The man and woman could make out they were being followed, and had redoubled their speed. D'Artagnan hastened on, overtook them and stopped before them.

"What do you want, sir?" demanded the Musketeer, drawing back a step, and with a foreign accent.

"I don't have anything to do with you, sir," said D'Artagnan. "It is with Madame here."

"With Madame! You do not know her!" replied the stranger.

"You are mistaken, sir; I know her very well."

The Musketeer advanced a step or two and pushed D'Artagnan aside with his hand.

D'Artagnan jumped backwards, and drew his sword.

At the same time, with the rapidity of lightning the unknown drew his.

"In the name of Heaven, my lord!" cried Madame Bonacieux, throwing herself between the two men.

"My lord!" cried D'Artagnan, enlightened by a sudden idea, "my lord! Pardon me, sir, but are you not ..."

"My lord, the Duke of Buckingham!" informed Madame Bonacieux. "And you are putting us all in danger by stopping us. Follow us at a distance of twenty paces to the Louvre, and if any one watches us, kill him!"

CHAPTER 7

Duke of Buckingham

Madame Bonacieux and the Duke entered the Louvre without difficulty. Everyone knew that Madame Bonacieux worked for the Queen, while the Duke was wearing the uniform of the Musketeers of M. de Tréville, who were on guard that evening.

Madame Bonacieux took Buckingham to a private room, unlocked the door, and pushed him inside. "Remain here, my Lord Duke; someone will come." Then she went out of the same door and locked it again. The Duke was now virtually a prisoner.

Nevertheless, the Duke of Buckingham did not experience an instant of fear. He was brave, rash, and enterprising. He had learned that the message that had brought him to Paris was actually a trap. But, instead of returning to England, he had decided that he would not leave without seeing the Queen. The Queen had at first positively refused; but at last she had decided to see him and insist on his immediate departure.

Left alone, Buckingham walked towards a mirror. At the age of thirty-five, the Duke could have been rightly called the most handsome and the most elegant gentleman of France or England, who had dazzled the beautiful and proud Anne of Austria, making her fall in love with him.

A moment later, a door hidden in the tapestry opened, and a woman appeared. As Buckingham saw her image in the glass, he uttered a cry. It was the Queen.

Buckingham threw himself at the feet of Anne of Austria, and before she could prevent him, he kissed the hem of her robe.

"Duke, you already know that I did not write to you," said the Queen. "The Cardinal has set up a trap. If you are caught, my honour will be at stake."

"Yes, yes, Madame!" cried the Duke.

"My lord, I want to tell you that we must never see each other again. Duke, leave me—go. Go, I beg you!" pleaded Anne of Austria.

"I will leave; but please give me something— a ring, a necklace, a chain… which will always remind me of you!"

The Queen went into her apartment, and came out holding a casket in her hand. The casket was made of rosewood and had her monogram inscribed in gold. It contained twelve diamond studs set on a blue ribbon and tied into a bow.

"Here, my lord," said she; "keep this in memory of me."

Buckingham took the casket, and fell a second time on his knees.

"You promised me you would go back," said the Queen.

"And I keep my word. Within six months, if I am not dead, I shall see you again, even if I have to upset the whole world for it."

And he took leave of his beloved.

Madame Bonacieux led the Duke out of the palace, to where his coach was standing hidden. His coach took him to the coast, from where he left for England.

CHAPTER 8

The Man of Meung

The officers who had arrested M. Bonacieux, conducted him straight to the Bastille and questioned him about his wife.

"They have abducted her, Monsieur," cried Bonacieux.

"And do you know the man who has committed this deed?" asked an officer.

"I suspect," said he, "a tall, dark man, of lofty carriage. If I saw him again, I would recognise him even among a thousand persons."

On hearing this, the face of the officer grew dark and he ordered Bonacieux to be taken away to his cell. Then, he hastily wrote a letter and dispatched it.

In the evening, Bonacieux was taken out of the prison in a carriage to another house. There, an officer of pleasant appearance took him to a large and closed room. A man of middle height, with a thin face, piercing eyes, a broad brow and a proud, haughty bearing was standing before the fireplace. This man was the Cardinal Richelieu - the most eminent and powerful man in France.

"Is this Bonacieux?" asked he, after a moment of silence.

"Yes, Monseigneur," replied the officer.

"Very well, please leave us alone now."

After the officer had left, the Cardinal turned to Bonacieux, and looked at him with his sharp and piercing eyes.

At the end of ten minutes of examination, the Cardinal murmured, "No, he is not capable of conspiracy."

Then, aloud, he said, "You are charged with plotting against France, along with your wife and the Duke of Buckingham!"

"No, Monseigneur, I am innocent!" cried Bonacieux.

"Your wife has escaped. Did you know that?"

"No, Monseigneur."

"When you would bring your wife from the Louvre, did you always return directly home?"

"No; as she had business with linen-drapers, I rarely escorted her to those shops."

The Cardinal talked to him for a while, offered him a bag full of gold, and asked him to be his ally. Once he was assured that Bonacieux was on his side, he set him free.

After this, the Cardinal went to see the King. He was aware of the King's suspicions and prejudices

against the Queen, and often took advantage of this prejudice.

The Cardinal told him, "Sir, Buckingham has been in Paris for five days, and left it only this morning. Are you certain that the Queen and he did not see each other?"

Hearing these words, Louis XIII grew pale and red alternately.

"I believe the Queen has a high sense of

her duty, sir. Well there is a simple way to make sure."

"What is that?"

"Give a ball; you know how much the Queen loves dancing. By the way, sir," the Cardinal added, "do not forget to tell her Majesty that you would like to see her wearing her diamond studs."

Louis XIII was struck with surprise when the Cardinal mentioned the diamond studs, and began to imagine that this suggestion concealed some mystery. Then he went to the Queen, and as usual, started accusing her. "But," cried Anne of Austria, tired of these vague attacks, "but, sir, what have I done? Let me know what crime I have committed."

"Madame," he said, composing himself, "there will shortly be a ball at the City Hall. I wish for you to appear at it in the state dress, and particularly ornamented with the diamond studs which I gave you on your birthday. That is my answer. You hear, Madame?"

"Yes, sir, I hear," stammered the Queen.

With this, the King left. The queen, thinking of her misfortune, broke out into sobs and tears.

"Can I be of no service to your Majesty?" said a voice full of sweetness and pity.

The Queen turned round quickly. At one of the doors which opened into the Queen's apartment, appeared the pretty Madame Bonacieux.

"The King speaks of those studs which you gave to the Duke of Buckingham, did you not?" she said. "Those studs were in a little rosewood box, which he held under his arm? Is it not so, Madame?"

"Yes."

"Well," continued Madame Bonacieux, "we must have those studs back again."

"Someone must be sent to the Duke."

"Have confidence in me, Madame. I will find a messenger."

"Oh! I must write a letter to him requesting him to give me back the diamonds."

"Oh yes; that is very important. A letter written by Your Majesty, and bearing your own private seal."

Anne of Austria ran to her jewel-case.

"Here," said she, "here is a ring of great value, as I have been told. It came from my brother, the King of Spain. It is mine, and I can dispose of it if I want. Take this ring, and turn it into money."

She handed Constance the ring and the letter addressed, "To my Lord, Duke of Buckingham, London," and asked her to find a messenger. Constance Bonacieux was home after ten minutes. She saw that her husband was home but was unaware that he was now a friend of the Cardinal.

Madame Bonacieux offered him her forehead to kiss.

"Let us talk a little," she said.

"About what?" asked Bonacieux.

"I have something very important to tell you."

"Speak, then."

"You must set out immediately. I will give you a paper with which you must not part on any account, and which you will deliver into the proper hands."

"And where am I to go?"

"London. A well-known person sends you, a well-known person awaits you."

"Thank you, Madame; I am aware of everything now and I refuse to take your orders. The Cardinal has told me everything."

"The Cardinal?" cried Madame Bonacieux. "Have you seen the Cardinal?"

"He sent for me," Bonacieux answered, proudly. "He gave me his hand, and he called me his friend—his friend! Do you hear that, Madame? I am a friend of the great Cardinal!"

Madame Bonacieux was too surprised to say anything. Bonacieux kissed his wife's hand and set off to see a friend.

As Constance was wondering whom she

could send as the Queen's messenger to London, she heard a rap on the ceiling, which made her raise her head.

She heard a voice which reached her through the ceiling, "Dear Madame Bonacieux, open the little side door for me, and I will come down to you."

"Ah, Madame," said D'Artagnan, as he entered by the door which the young woman had opened for him, "allow me to tell you that you have a sorry husband there."

"Then you overheard our conversation?" asked Madame Bonacieux uneasily.

"The whole of it. And I understand that the Queen wants a brave, intelligent and devoted man to make a journey to London for her."

Madame Bonacieux made no reply, but her heart beat with joy, and a secret hope shone in her eyes.

"Speak! Command! What must I do?" said D'Artagnan.

"Listen," said she; "I swear to you, before God who hears us, that if you betray me, I will kill myself and accuse you of my death."

Then, the young woman confided to D'Artagnan the terrible secret. "But still there is another thing," said Madame Bonacieux.

"What is that?" asked D'Artagnan, seeing that Madame Bonacieux hesitated to proceed.

"You have, perhaps, no money?"

"Perhaps is too much," said D'Artagnan, smiling.

Constance went to the cupboard, took out a bag of money and gave it to D'Artagnan. D'Artagnan accepted the money, said goodbye to Madame Bonacieux and set out on his mission.

Meanwhile, Madame Bonacieux fell on her knees, and clasping her hands, cried, "Oh, my God! Protect the Queen, protect me!"

"Believe me, in these kinds of ventures four must set out, for one to reach."

"Ah, you are right, sir," said D'Artagnan. "For that you have to give leave to Athos, Porthos and Aramis as well."

So, Tréville wrote out four passes and gave them to D'Artagnan, who thanked him, took his leave, and set out to find his friends.

At two o'clock in the morning, the four adventurers left Paris. The lackeys followed, armed to the teeth. All went well as far as Chantilly, where they arrived at about eight o'clock in the morning. They stopped at an inn for breakfast.

As they were rising from the table after their breakfast, a stranger approached Porthos and proposed they drink a toast to the Cardinal's health.

"Certainly I would, if only you would drink to the King's health?" said Porthos.

"I acknowledge no other King but his Eminence," cried the stranger, and drew his sword ready for a fight.

Porthos, too, was ready with his sword.

"Kill your man, and rejoin us as soon as you can," Athos told Porthos.

Then the three said goodbye to Porthos and continued with their journey.

After a while, they reached a place where the road was confined between two high banks. Some people were digging holes and making muddy potholes.

Suddenly, the labourers rushed towards the ditch and took out muskets which had been hidden there.

"It is an ambush!" shouted D'Artagnan, "don't waste a shot! Forward!" The friends were successful in getting away safely. However, as they were trying to escape, Aramis was hit by a bullet, and after travelling for some time he could proceed no further. He grew paler every minute, and so his friends took him to an inn in Crevecoeur, and left Bazin with him. The original party of eight was now reduced to four. D'Artagnan and Athos arrived in Amiens, and alighted at the inn of the Golden Lily to spend the night.

Grimaud was set to guard the horses while Planchet slept in front of the door so that D'Artagnan and Athos wouldn't be taken by surprise. At four o'clock in the morning, the two friends heard a terrible noise in the stables. On investigation, they discovered Grimaud lying unconscious with a bleeding head. Planchet was immediately sent to saddle the horses, but they were still too exhausted to go any further.

Athos and D'Artagnan went out, and at the door, they saw two horses, fresh, strong and fully equipped. These were just what they wanted. Upon asking where their owners were, they were informed that the men were settling their bills with the master.

Athos went down to pay the money, while D'Artagnan and Planchet stood at the street door. Athos was shown a low room at the back where the host was sitting. Athos entered, and took out two pistoles to pay the bill.

The host was alone. He took the money which Athos offered to him, and after turning it repeatedly in his hands, suddenly cried out, "This is forged, I will have you and your friends arrested for this."

"You rogue!" cried Athos, stepping towards him, "Don't try to trick me or I'll cut your ears off!"

The host stooped, took two pistols from the half-open drawer, pointed them at Athos, and called out for help. At the same instant, four armed men entered by side doors, and rushed upon Athos.

"I am captured!" shouted Athos, as loudly as he could. "Get away, D'Artagnan!"

D'Artagnan and Planchet did not require twice bidding. They unfastened the two horses that were waiting at the door, leaped upon them and set off at full gallop.

After they had finally reached the port, Planchet called his master's attention to a gentleman who had just arrived with his lackey, and who was about fifty paces ahead of them. His boots were covered with dust, and he was asking whether he could instantly cross over to England.

"An order arrived this morning that no one was allowed to cross without the Cardinal's permission," said the captain of a vessel that was ready to set sail.

"I have that permission," replied the gentleman, drawing a paper from his pocket, "here it is."

"Have it signed by the governor of the port," said the captain.

"Very well," said the gentleman.

And with his lackey, he started for the governor's country house.

D'Artagnan and Planchet followed the gentleman at a distance of five hundred paces. Once outside the city, D'Artagnan quickly overtook the gentleman as he was entering a little wood.

"Planchet," called out D'Artagnan, "take care of the lackey while I will manage the master."

The gentleman drew his sword and sprang upon D'Artagnan; but he had to deal with a tough customer. In three seconds, D'Artagnan had wounded him three times. At the third thrust, the gentleman fell like a log and fainted.

D'Artagnan searched his pockets, and took from one of them the order for the passage. It was in the name of the Comte de Wardes.

"Come, Planchet," said D'Artagnan, "now to the governor's house."

The governor signed the passport and delivered it to D'Artagnan, who thanked the governor, bowed, and departed.

The vessel was quite ready to sail, and the captain was waiting on the port.

"Well?" said he, on seeing D'Artagnan.

"Here is my signed pass," said the latter.

"And that other gentleman?"

"He will not go today," said D'Artagnan, "but

here, I'll pay you for us."

"In that case let us start then," said the captain.

D'Artagnan leaped with Planchet into the boat. They were on board after five minutes. And the next morning, they reached Dover, England.

D'Artagnan did not know one word of English. So he wrote the name of Buckingham on a piece of paper, and every one to whom he showed it pointed out to him the way to the Duke's palace.

They inquired for the Duke on their arrival at the castle; and Patrick, who was the Duke's confidential valet, informed them that he was hunting hawks with the King.

Patrick galloped off, reached the Duke, and announced to him that a messenger from France awaited him.

Buckingham, suspecting that something was going on in France, put his horse into a gallop, and rode straight up to D'Artagnan.

"Has any misfortune happened to the Queen?" cried Buckingham.

"I believe not. Nevertheless, I believe she is in some great threat from which your Grace alone can rescue her."

"I!" cried Buckingham. "What is it?"

"Take this letter," said D'Artagnan.

The Duke broke the seal, read the letter, and cried, "Patrick, join the King, wherever he may be, and tell his Majesty that I humbly beg him to excuse me, as I have to go to London immediately. Come, sir, come!"

CHAPTER 10

The Diamond Studs

As they rode along, D'Artagnan told the Duke all that he himself knew. It surprised the Duke that someone so young could be so brave and resourceful.

The horses went like the wind, and they were soon at the gates of London. On entering the court of his palace, Buckingham sprang from his horse, and ran towards the staircase. The Duke walked so fast that D'Artagnan had some trouble in keeping up with him. They then found themselves in a small chapel covered with a tapestry of Persian silk, embossed with gold, and brilliantly lit with a vast number of wax candles. Over a kind of altar, was a life-size portrait of Anne of Austria. And beneath the portrait, was the casket containing the diamond studs.

The Duke approached the altar; fell on his knees, then opened the casket.

"Here," said he, drawing from the casket a large bow of blue ribbon all sparkling with diamonds, "here are the precious studs."

All of a sudden, he uttered a terrible cry.

"What is the matter?" exclaimed D'Artagnan anxiously; "what has happened to you, my lord?"

"All is lost! All is lost!" cried Buckingham, turning as pale as death; "two of the studs are missing – there are only ten of them left!"

"Could you have lost them, my lord?"

"No, they have been stolen, and it is the Cardinal who has dealt me this blow. See! The ribbons which held them have been cut with scissors. Let me remember, the only time I wore these studs was at a ball given by the King a week ago at Windsor. Milady de Winter was with me at that ball. The woman is an agent of the Cardinal!"

The Duke then asked his valet to summon his jeweller.

"Master O'Reilly," said the Duke when the goldsmith entered, leading him into the chapel. "Look at these diamond studs, and tell me what they are worth apiece."

The goldsmith cast a glance at the elegant manner in which they were set, and without hesitation, replied, "Fifteen hundred pistoles each, your Grace."

"How many days would it require to make two studs exactly like them?"

"A week, your Grace."

"I will give you three thousand pistoles each if I can have them by the day after tomorrow."

"Your Grace, you shall have them."

With this, the goldsmith left.

An hour later, the Duke passed an order in London that no vessel bound for France should leave the ports—not even the packet boat with letters. In the eyes of everybody, this was a declaration of war between the two kingdoms – England and France!

On the day after the next, by eleven o'clock, the two diamond studs were finished. They were exact imitations of the other ten and it was difficult to distinguish them from the originals.

Buckingham immediately called D'Artagnan.

"Here," said Buckingham, "are the diamond studs that you came to fetch. Go to the port, ask for the ship Le Sund, and give this letter to the captain. He will convey you to a little port where certainly no one is going to watch for you."

D'Artagnan bowed to the Duke, and quickly made his way to the port opposite the Tower of London. He found the vessel that had been named to him, delivered his letter to the captain, and they set sail at once.

CHAPTER 11

The Ballet

The next day, nothing was talked of in Paris but the ball which the provosts of the city were to give to the King and Queen. The King was dressed in an elegant hunting costume, and the other nobles were dressed as he was.

Meanwhile, the Cardinal drew near to the King and placed a casket in his hand. The King opened it, and found in it two diamond studs.

"What does this mean?" demanded he of the Cardinal.

"Nothing," replied the Cardinal; "only, if the Queen has the studs – but I very much doubt if she has – count them, sir, and if you find only ten, ask her Majesty who could have stolen them from her."

Suddenly, a cry of admiration burst from every mouth.

The Queen had made her entrance. Anne of Austria was assuredly the most beautiful woman in France. She wore a beaver hat with blue feathers; and on her left shoulder, on a blue ribbon tied into a bow, sparkled the diamond studs.

On seeing them, the King trembled with joy and the Cardinal with anger.

The Queen had them; the only question was, had she ten or twelve?

At that moment, the violins sounded the signal for the ballet. The King advanced towards the hostess, Madame la Présidente, and the host, towards the Queen. They took their places, and the ballet began.

The King danced facing the Queen, and every time that he passed by her he devoured with his eyes the diamond studs; he could not make out the number of them.

Meanwhile, a cold sweat covered the Cardinal's brow.

The ballet lasted an hour. When the ballet ended, the whole gathering applauded and the King hastened to the Queen.

"I thank you, Madame," said he, "for the deference you have shown to my wishes; but I think two of your studs are missing, and I bring them back to you."

At these words, he held out to the Queen the two studs the Cardinal had given him.

"How, sir?" cried the young Queen, with surprise; "you are giving me, then, two more! So now, I shall have fourteen."

The King counted them, and there were indeed twelve studs on Her Majesty's shoulder.

The King called the Cardinal to him.

"What does this mean, Cardinal?" asked the King, in a severe tone.

"This means, sir," replied the Cardinal, "that I was desirous of presenting Her Majesty with these two studs, and that I didn't dare to present them to her myself; so I gave them to you."

"Oh thank you so much, I am very grateful to you," replied Anne of Austria with a smile that proved to the Cardinal she hadn't been fooled by his gallantry.

Then, after bowing to the King and the Cardinal, the Queen proceeded to her chamber.

D'Artagnan, after his task had been completed, was about to leave, when he felt a light touch on his shoulder. He turned round, and saw a young woman, who signalled to him to follow her. He at once recognised his usual guide, the cheerful and witty Madame Bonacieux. She opened the door of a closet, which was entirely dark, and led the young man into it. Then, opening a second door, she disappeared.

The young man stood in the shadow and waited as he heard voices on the other side of the door. Several times he heard the word 'Majesty' being repeated and then he could distinguish the voice of the Queen herself.

At last, an arm, surpassingly beautiful in appearance, suddenly glided through a tapestry. D'Artagnan understood that this was his reward. He cast himself on his knees, took hold of the hand, and touched it respectfully with his lips; then the hand was withdrawn, leaving in his hand a ring. The door closed immediately, and D'Artagnan found himself again in complete darkness.

D'Artagnan had received the reward of his devotion. He placed the ring on his finger, and left.

CHAPTER 12

The Rendezvous

D'Artagnan went home immediately. Although it was after three o'clock in the morning, and he had the worst quarters of Paris to pass through, he met with no misadventure. He found the door of his passage open, sprang up the stairs, and knocked softly, in a manner agreed upon between him and his lackey.

Planchet, whom he had sent home two hours

before from the City Hall, came and opened the door.

"Has any one brought a letter for me?" asked D'Artagnan, eagerly.

"No one has brought a letter, sir," replied Planchet; "but I found one that came by itself."

"What do you mean by that, you stupid fellow?"

"I mean that when I came in, although I had the key of your apartment in my pocket, I found a letter on the green table-cover in your bedroom."

"And where is that letter?"

"I left it where I found it, sir."

D'Artagnan went into his chamber and opened the letter. It was from Madame Bonacieux, and it read:

"I offer you my warm thanks. Meet at St. Cloud today evening about ten o'clock, in front of the pavilion at the corner of M. d'Estrées's hotel C.B."

D'Artagnan's joy knew no bounds on reading the letter.

He took a couple of hours sleep, got up at seven o'clock in the morning and took his way towards M. de Tréville's hotel. He found M. de Tréville in a most joyful mood. The King and Queen had been charming to him at the ball. The Cardinal, however, had been particularly ill-tempered.

"Now," said M. de Tréville, lowering his voice and looking round at every corner of the apartment to see whether they were alone – "now let us talk about you, my young friend; it is evident that your lucky return has something to do with the King's joy, the Queen's triumph, and the Cardinal's humiliation. You must be careful."

"What do I have to fear," replied D'Artagnan, "as long as I have the good fortune to enjoy their Majesties' favour?"

"Everything, believe me. By the way," resumed M. de Tréville, "what has happened to your three companions?"

"I was about to ask you if you had heard any news of them."

"No, my young friend."

"Well, I left Porthos at Chantilly, with a duel on his hands; Aramis at Crèvecoeur, with a bullet in his shoulder; while Athos was detained at Amiens."

"By God!" said M. de Tréville. "And how did you escape?"

"By a miracle, sir, I must acknowledge."

"In your place, I would do one thing," said Tréville.

"What, sir?"

"While his Eminence was looking for me in Paris, I should secretly take the road to Picardy, and go and make some enquiries regarding my three companions."

"Your advice is good, sir, and I will set out tomorrow."

"Tomorrow! And why not this evening?" asked

Tréville.

"This evening, sir, I have an urgent business in Paris," replied D'Artagnan.

"Ah, young man, it's surely some love affair!" exclaimed Tréville. "But take my advice and set out this evening."

"But I have given my word, sir."

"Well then, would you or your companions require money?"

"I still have fifty pistoles. We left Paris each with seventy-five pistoles in our pocket."

"Well, a pleasant journey to you, then."

"Thank you, sir."

And D'Artagnan left M. de Tréville, touched more than ever by his paternal care for his Musketeers.

At nine o'clock that evening, D'Artagnan picked his sword and placed two pistols in his belt; then he mounted his horse and departed quietly. It was quite dark, and no one saw him go out. He reached the appointed place and waited for

Madame Bonacieux. His eyes were fixed upon a house situated at the angle of the wall. All the windows of the house were closed with shutters, except one on the first storey.

D'Artagnan saw a group of trees in front of the window. He climbed one of the trees, and in an instant was among the branches. As his eyes penetrated through the clear glass into the interior of the porch, he saw an alarming scene: one of the panes of glass was broken; the door of the room was open, while a table set with dinner lay overturned in the middle of the room. Everything in the apartment gave evidence of a violent and desperate struggle!

D'Artagnan hastened down into the street, his heart throbbing frightfully.

Outside, on the ground, he saw hoof-marks all over the place. He also noticed the wheels of a carriage, which had made a deep impression in the soft earth; it seemed to have returned towards Paris.

After looking around for some time, D'Artagnan found a woman's torn glove near the wall. D'Artagnan became almost frantic and ran up to the small cottage that was in front of the house. The gate was locked, but he leaped over the hedge, and in spite of the barking of a chained dog, went up to the cabin.

There was no answer to his first knocking. A deathlike silence reigned in the cottage as in the house; but as the cottage was his last resource, he kept knocking.

Soon, he heard a slight noise within. A window opened and an old man's face appeared, but closed again as soon as the light from a small lamp fell upon D'Artagnan's sword and pistol.

"In the name of Heaven," he cried, "listen to me! I have been waiting for someone who has not come. I am dying with anxiety. Has any misfortune happened in the neighbourhood? Please tell me!"

The window was opened again slowly, and

the same face reappeared only it was paler than before.

D'Artagnan related his story simply, with the omission of names. He told how he had an appointment with a young woman before that house, and how, seeing she did not come, he had climbed the tree, and by the lamplight had seen the disorder of the room.

The old man read so much truth and so much grief in the young man's face that he made a sign to listen, and speaking in a low voice, said, "It was about nine o'clock when I heard a noise in the street. I went and opened the gate, and saw three men dressed as cavaliers. They had a coach with horses, and some saddle-horses. They asked me for a ladder, paid me a crown for it, and asked me not to speak about it to anybody."

"Well, then, after I had shut the gate behind them, I immediately went out through a back door and positioned myself under a clump of trees; from there I could see everything without being seen."

"The three men brought the carriage up quietly, and took out of it a little, short, stout, elderly man, poorly dressed in dark-coloured clothes. He climbed the ladder very carefully, looked slyly in at the window of the porch, came down as quietly as he had gone up, and whispered, "It is she!" "Immediately, one man went inside through the porch door, while two climbed up the ladder. All at once a woman screamed loudly in the room, and then ran to the window and opened it, as if to throw herself out of it. After that I didn't see anything, but I heard the noise of breaking furniture. The woman screamed and cried for help, but her cries were soon stifled. Two of the men carried her to the carriage; the little old man entered it after her. The carriage went off at a rapid pace, escorted by the three horsemen, and all was over. From that moment, I have neither seen nor heard anything."

D'Artagnan was shocked by such terrible

news. He remained motionless and mute.

"Can you describe," cried he, "the man who headed this infernal expedition?"

"A tall, dark man, with dark eyes and a scar on his temple," replied the old man.

"That's the man!" cried D'Artagnan, "Again he, forever he! He is my demon!"

With a broken heart, D'Artagnan made his way toward the ferry. His mind was torn by doubt, grief, and despair.

"Oh, if I had my three friends here," cried he, "I should have, at least, some hopes of finding her; but who knows what has become of them?"

It was almost midnight by then, and D'Artagnan decided to pass the night in an inn.

CHAPTER 13

Porthos, Aramis and the Wife of Athos

The next morning, instead of returning directly home, D'Artagnan went to M. de Tréville's door and related everything to him. M. de Tréville was at once certain that all of it was the doing of the Cardinal and asked D'Artagnan to leave Paris, as soon as possible.

So, D'Artagnan and Planchet rode out of the

city separately, agreeing to meet at Chantilly. They arrived there without any accident, and alighted at the hotel of St. Martin, the same they had stopped at on their first trip.

The host informed them that Porthos was still there, but had been injured while fighting a duel. D'Artagnan rushed upstairs to see his friend. Porthos was in bed; and at the sight of D'Artagnan, uttered a loud cry of joy.

At that moment, Planchet entered. He informed his master that the horses were sufficiently refreshed, and they could set out on their journey.

D'Artagnan, reassured with regard to Porthos, now grew anxious to obtain news of his two other friends. He held out his hand to Porthos and left to resume his journey, saying that he would return in about eight days.

D'Artagnan and Planchet passed through six or eight leagues before they reached the inn where they had left Aramis.

A hostess received them.

D'Artagnan asked her if she knew anything about Aramis.

"Well, sir, he is still here," replied the hostess, and asked him to knock at room Number Five on the second floor.

D'Artagnan rushed in the direction pointed out, turned the handle of the door Number Five, and went into the chamber.

Aramis was overwhelmed with joy to see his friend.

"Good-afternoon to you, dear D'Artagnan," said Aramis. "Believe me, I am very glad to see you."

"Now we still have to get news of Athos," said D'Artagnan, reassured at seeing his friend sufficiently recovered.

The next morning, D'Artagnan took leave of Aramis, after entrusting him to the care of Bazin and the hostess.

About eleven o'clock in the morning he and

Planchet were at the door of the inn where they had left Athos.

Remembering that the innkeeper had unjustly detained Athos, D'Artagnan was filled with fresh indignation and anger when he arrived. The innkeeper, frightened at the young man's wrath, begged to be listened to. He explained that he had been forewarned by the authorities that some men who were criminals disguised as Musketeers were expected in the neighbourhood. He had received a description of their uniforms, their servants, and their facial features. And thus, he had tried to detain them. The innkeeper told D'Artagnan that Athos killed one of the men in the inn and seriously wounded two more; then he barricaded himself in the basement and threatened to kill anyone who tried to get near him. The innkeeper had gone to the police, but they wouldn't help him because the instructions concerning the fraudulent Musketeers did not come from them. They refused to arrest someone who might be one of the King's Musketeers.

Athos had remained in the basement, and had drunk over a hundred and fifty bottles of wine, and eaten all the hams and sausages in the basement. The innkeeper lamented that he was almost ruined.

D'Artagnan rushed to see Athos.

Athos gave him a warm welcome. D'Artagnan then related to him how he had found Porthos and Aramis. As he finished, the landlord entered with wine and ham.

"Good!" said Athos, filling his glass and D'Artagnan's. "Here's to Porthos and Aramis! But, my friend, what is the matter with you, and what has happened to you personally? You don't look happy."

"Alas!" said D'Artagnan, "It is because I am the most unfortunate of all."

"You, unfortunate?" said Athos.

"Presently," said D'Artagnan.

D'Artagnan then related his adventure with Madame Bonacieux. Athos listened to him without moving a muscle. His dull eye flashed for an instant, and then it became dull and vacant as before.

"Your misfortune is laughable," said Athos, shrugging his shoulders. "Let me tell you a real tale of love."

"I am all attention. Please start," said D'Artagnan.

"A friend of mine—please keep this in mind, a friend of mine, not myself," said Athos, "fell in love with a sixteen year old girl. She was beautiful as an angel. She lived in a small town with her brother, who was a vicar. Both had recently come into the country. My friend, who was a Count, was an honourable man, and he married her."

"Well, one day when she was hunting with her husband, she fell from her horse and fainted. The Count ran to her help. As her sleeves slipped off, it laid bare her shoulder."

"Guess," said Athos, with a loud burst of laughter, "guess what she had on her shoulder… A fleur-de-lis! She was branded!"

"The truth, my friend, was that the angel was a demon. The young girl had been a thief!"

"And what did the Count do?" asked D'Artagnan.

"The Count was a great noble and had on his estates the right of life and death. He tied her hands behind her, and hanged her on a tree!"

"Heavens, Athos, a murder!" cried D'Artagnan.

"Yes, a murder—nothing else," said Athos, pale as death.

Then he let his head fall on his two hands, while D'Artagnan sat facing him, overwhelmed with dismay.

"That has cured me of beautiful and loving women," said Athos, getting to his feet.

"And her brother?" asked D'Artagnan, timidly.

"Oh, I inquired after him for the purpose of hanging him likewise; but – he had left the curacy instantly."

"Was it ever known who this miserable fellow was?"

"He was, without a doubt, the lady's first lover and accomplice."

D'Artagnan could no longer bear this conversation, which was driving him crazy. He let his head fall on his hands and pretended to go to sleep. Athos and D'Artagnan's only anxiety now was to depart. Before leaving, they left Athos' old horse with the innkeeper to compensate his losses.

The two soon arrived at Crévecoeur. Aramis paid his bill, and then the three set forward to join Porthos.

They found him better than before. All four of them left for Paris. On arriving in Paris, D'Artagnan found a letter from M. de Tréville. Tréville informed him that, at his request, the King had just promised him D'Artagnan's immediate admission into the Musketeers.

As this was the height of D'Artagnan's worldly ambition, he ran, full of joy, to seek his comrades, whom he had left only half an hour before, and gave them the happy news.

CHAPTER 14

Milady

One day, not long after, D'Artagnan saw a lady whose beauty held his eyes. Then, he realised that she was the same lady whom the man from Meung had addressed as Milady.

As it was quite possible that the man from Meung had carried off Constance Bonacieux, D'Artagnan decided to follow Milady, as both seemed to know each other quite well. He saw her get into her carriage, and heard her order the coachman to drive to St. Germain.

As it was useless for one on foot to try and keep pace with a carriage drawn by two powerful horses, D'Artagnan returned home. Then he and Planchet got into their saddles, and took the road to St. Germain. Arriving at St. Germain, D'Artagnan rode along a very quiet street, when he spied Milady's coach ahead of him.

D'Artagnan followed the coach.

After a while, the carriage stopped. Milady put her charming fair head out at the window, and gave some orders to her maid. D'Artagnan followed the maid with his eyes, and saw her going towards the courtyard of a house decorated beautifully with flowers.

Suddenly, D'Artagnan saw a man's face peeping out from a window of the house.

Planchet recognized him at once.

It was the same man with whom Planchet

had fought - the lackey of the Comte de Wardes whom D'Artagnan had fought and defeated.

That meant the house belonged to the Comte de Wardes!

D'Artagnan told Planchet to find out whether the Count was alive. Planchet headed towards the house, and there, met Milady's maid. She mistook him for the lackey of the master of the house, and handed out a little note to him, saying, "For your master."

Then she returned to the carriage.

Planchet turned the note repeatedly; then, he handed it over to D'Artagnan, saying, "This is for you."

"For me?" cried D'Artagnan. "Are you sure?"

"Yes, the maid said it was for my master. And only you are my master." D'Artagnan opened the letter and read it: in the note Milady had asked for a rendezvous.

"Well done, Planchet! Now jump up on your horse, and let us overtake the carriage."

After following Milady's carriage for five minutes, they saw the carriage drawn up by the roadside. A cavalier, richly dressed, was close to the coach door.

The conversation between Milady and the cavalier was so animated that D'Artagnan stopped on the other side of the carriage. No one but the pretty maid saw him. The conversation took place in English – a language which D'Artagnan could not understand. But by the accent, he could make out that the beautiful Englishwoman was in a great rage. The cavalier broke into a loud laugh, which appeared to infuriate Milady.

D'Artagnan thought this was the right moment to interfere. He approached the carriage, and, taking off his hat respectfully, said, "Madame, this cavalier seems to have made you very angry. Speak one word, Madame, and I will punish him for his lack of courtesy."

At the first word, Milady turned round, looking at the young man in astonishment. When he had finished, she said, in very good French, "Sir, I would have placed myself under your protection, if the person who is picking a quarrel with me were not my brother."

"Ah, excuse me, then," said D'Artagnan; "you must be aware that I was ignorant of that, Madame."

Milady offered her thanks to him and invited him to pay her a visit at Number Six Palace Royale. Then she threw herself back in her carriage, and called out coolly to the coachman, "Drive home!"

The pretty maid cast an uneasy glance at D'Artagnan. His good looks seemed to have made an impression on her.

The next day, D'Artagnan visited Milady de Winter.

Milady offered him a warm welcome, and a cheerful conversation started between them. The person who had quarrelled with her on the road was also present. She introduced D'Artagnan to him. He was Lord Winter, her brother-in-law.

After a while, Lord Winter took leave of them.

Milady told D'Artagnan that she had married a younger brother of the family, who had left her a widow with one child. If Lord Winter did not marry, this child would remain Lord Winter's sole heir. After half an hour's conversation, D'Artagnan took leave of Milady.

D'Artagnan left the parlour the happiest of men. He was gradually falling in love with the fascinatingly beautiful woman. On the stairs, he met the pretty maid who brushed gently against him as she passed, and then, blushing to the eyes, asked his pardon.

D'Artagnan came on the next day again, and Milady received him with more warmth and friendliness than on the day before. Lord Winter was not at home. Milady appeared to take a great interest in him and asked him where he was from, who were his friends, and whether he had ever been to England.

D'Artagnan replied that he had been sent there once by M. de Tréville to bargain for some new horses.

When it was quite late in the evening, D'Artagnan left.

D'Artagnan came again on the next day and the day after that, and each day Milady gave him a more gracious welcome. Every evening, either at the entrance, in the corridor, or on the stairs, he met the pretty maid, Kitty; but D'Artagnan never paid any attention to her.

In spite of the warnings of his conscience and the wise counsels of Athos, D'Artagnan, hour by hour, fell more deeply in love with Milady. And, at the same time, Kitty had fallen deeply in love with D'Artagnan.

CHAPTER 15

Maid and Mistress

One day, when D'Artagnan arrived as usual at Milady lodgings, he found Kitty at the gateway of the hotel.

"I should like to speak a few words with you," stammered the maid.

"Speak, my dear, speak," said D'Artagnan; "what is it that you want to tell me?"

"If Monsieur would follow me?" said Kitty

timidly, and led him to her room.

This room communicated with Milady's by another door.

Then Kitty continued, "You love my mistress, very dearly?"

"Oh, more than I can say, Kitty! I am madly in love with her!"

"But, sir," replied Kitty, "my mistress does not love you at all."

"How can you say so?"

Kitty then handed D'Artagnan a note and asked him to read the address.

"THE COMTE DE WARDES."

D'Artagnan remembered the scene at St. Germain and quickly tore open the letter. It read:

"You have not answered my first note. Are you ill, or have you forgotten the glances you favoured me with at the ball of Mme. de Guise? You have an opportunity now, Count; do not let it go."

As he read it, D'Artagnan became very pale.

"I know what it is to be in love," said Kitty, in a voice full of compassion.

"You know what it is to be in love?" said D'Artagnan, looking at her for the first time with some interest.

Suddenly, the bell rang in Milady's chamber.

"Great Heavens!" cried Kitty, "My mistress is calling me!"

As Kitty rushed to her mistress, D'Artagnan rose, and, quickly opening the door of a large wardrobe, locked himself into it.

D'Artagnan could hear everything of Milady and Kitty's conversation through the communicating door, as it was left open.

"Well," Milady was saying, "I have not seen our Gascon this evening."

"Did he not come today?" said Kitty, "Has he found another lady already?"

"Oh no; he must have had some work," said Milady.

"What are you going to do with him,

Madame?"

"Do with him?" cried Milady. "Kitty, the Cardinal has lost his faith in me because of this man. I will take my revenge on him for that!"

"I thought you loved him," said Kitty.

"Love him? I detest him—he is a fool," answered Milady. "I should long ago have revenged myself on him if, and I don't know why, the Cardinal had not requested me to make peace with him."

D'Artagnan trembled to hear the menacing words from the lips of this charming creature.

"But you haven't made peace with the woman he was so fond of," said Kitty.

"What, the tradesman's wife? Has he not already forgotten her? That was a fine revenge!"

A cold sweat broke from D'Artagnan's brow.

"This woman is a monster!" he thought.

Meanwhile, Milady's toilette was finished and she left. D'Artagnan heard the door close, and then he opened the wardrobe door and came out. He thanked Kitty and left with a promise to return the next day.

That evening, when D'Artagnan left for Milady's lodgings, he had formed a little plan.

He found Kitty at the gate. She had been severely scolded by her mistress. Milady had charged her with negligence and had ordered her to come at nine o'clock in the morning to take a third letter to the Count.

D'Artagnan asked Kitty to promise him that she would bring him that letter. Kitty promised. She was madly in love with D'Artagnan and would do anything for him.

The next day, at eleven o'clock, D'Artagnan saw Kitty coming; she held in her hand a fresh note from Milady. It was for the Count. D'Artagnan opened the letter, and read as follows:

"This is the third time I have written to you to tell you that I love you. Remember that if I have to write a fourth time, it will be to tell you how much I detest you."

D'Artagnan coloured and grew pale several times, as he read this note.

Then he took a pen and wrote:

"Madame, until the present moment I could not believe that your two first letters were addressed to me, as I felt so unworthy of your love. But now I must believe that I have the good fortune to be loved by you. I will come at eleven o'clock this evening.

Comte de Wardes."

"There!" said the young man, handing Kitty the letter sealed and addressed.

"Give this note to Milady. It is the Comte de Wardes' reply."

Poor Kitty turned deathly pale: she suspected what the letter contained.

That evening about nine o'clock, D'Artagnan presented himself at Milady's house as usual. He found her in a charming humour. She had never before received him so kindly. The young Gascon saw at the first glance that his note had been delivered and was doing its work. At ten o'clock Milady began to appear uneasy. D'Artagnan realised that she was waiting for him to leave.

"She loves him devilishly," he murmured. Then he went out.

Kitty heard D'Artagnan enter her chamber.

At last, as the time for the interview with the Count drew near, Milady had all the lights extinguished, and dismissed Kitty with an order to bring in De Wardes the moment he arrived.

When D'Artagnan saw that the whole apartment was in darkness, he immediately sprang out from his hiding-place. Kitty was just closing the door.

"What is that noise?" asked Milady.

"It is I, the Comte de Wardes," replied D'Artagnan, in a whisper.

"Well," said Milady in a trembling voice, "Why do you not come in, Count? You know well that I am waiting for you."

At this appeal, D'Artagnan slipped into the

chamber. Both rage and jealousy gnawed his heart. He was angry at the wickedness of the woman, while her passionate speech towards another man aroused his jealousy.

"Yes, Count," said Milady, in her sweetest voice, "I am happy to obtain your love. I too love you. But take this, so that you may never forget me!"

She took a ring from her finger and gave it to D'Artagnan.

It was a magnificent sapphire encircled with diamonds.

Milady added, "You poor angel, whom that monster Gascon barely failed to kill. But be calm, I will take your revenge – a cruel revenge!"

Eventually, it was one o' clock and D'Artagnan took leave of Milady.

The next morning, D'Artagnan hastened to Athos' room and told him everything. Athos frowned more than once while D'Artagnan was talking.

Athos was gazing intently at the sapphire surrounded with diamonds, which D'Artagnan was wearing in place of the Queen's ring. "You are looking at my ring?" said the Gascon, proud of showing off such a rich gift before his friend.

"Yes," said Athos, "it reminds me of a family jewel."

"It is beautiful, isn't it?" said D'Artagnan.

"Magnificent!" replied Athos. "I did not know there were two such sapphires. Did you exchange it for your diamond?"

"No," said D'Artagnan, "it is a gift from Milady."

"This ring comes from Milady!" cried Athos in a tone which revealed great emotion. "Show me your ring, I beg you."

"Here it is," replied D'Artagnan, drawing it from his finger.

Athos examined the ring and grew very pale. Then he tried it on the ringfinger of his left hand. It fitted his finger as if it had been made for it. A shadow of anger and vengeance passed over the nobleman's brow.

"Do you know this ring?" said D'Artagnan.

"Let me look at that sapphire again," said Athos. "The one I just mentioned had one of its faces scratched by accident. Look, is it not strange?" and Athos pointed out to D'Artagnan the scratch on the ring.

"But from whom did this ring come to you, Athos?"

"From my mother; it is an old family jewel."

"And you--sold it?" asked D'Artagnan, hesitatingly.

"No," replied Athos, with a singular smile. "I gave it away as a token of love, as it has been given to you."

D'Artagnan became thoughtful in his turn. He took back the ring, but put it in his pocket and not on his finger.

"D'Artagnan," said Athos, taking his hand, "you know I love you; if I had a son I could not love him better. Take my advice, renounce this woman. There is something fatal about her."

"You are right," said D'Artagnan; "I accept that this woman terrifies me."

When he reached home, D'Artagnan found Kitty waiting for him. She was sent by her mistress to the false De Wardes. She wished to know when her lover would meet her again. And poor Kitty, pale and trembling, awaited D'Artagnan's reply.

He took a pen and wrote the following letter as his reply: "Do not depend upon me, Madame, for the next meeting. Since my recovery, I have numerous affairs on my hands that need immediate attention. I shall inform you once I am done with all of them. I kiss your hands. Comte de Wardes."

Kitty delivered the letter to her mistress, who opened it with a lot of eagerness. But on reading the first words, Milady was filled with fury. She crushed the paper in her hands and sank in a chair.

CHAPTER 16

Dream of Vengeance

That evening, Milady gave orders that M. D'Artagnan should be immediately admitted after his arrival. As nine o'clock was striking, D'Artagnan was at the Palace Royale.

Milady assumed the friendliest air possible, and talked with more than her usual brilliancy. Then she asked D'Artagnan if he had a lady love.

D'Artagnan, with the most sentimental air he

could assume, said, "From the moment I saw you; I have only breathed for you!"

Milady smiled with a strange smile.

"Then you do love me?" said she.

To this, D'Artagnan pledged his love to her for all time to come.

Milady thought for a while, and then said, "I have an enemy who has insulted me and it is war to the death between him and me. May I count on you as my ally?"

D'Artagnan at once understood what the cruel creature was aiming at.

"You may, Madame," said he, with emphasis. "My arm and my life are yours, as my love is. I am at your disposal."

"I love your devotion," said Milady.

And then she added very slowly, "His name is – De Wardes."

"Well, I will avenge you of this man," replied D'Artagnan. "But I really pity this poor Comte de Wardes, since he is not really as guilty towards you as he appears."

"Indeed?" said Milady, in an anxious tone. "Explain yourself."

So D'Artagnan revealed to her that it was he who had come as Comte de Wardes and that the ring she thought she had given to Comte de Wardes, was actually with him.

Pale and terrified, Milady started up and struck D'Artagnan with a violent blow on the chest. D'Artagnan held her back by her dress as she struggled to escape. Then the fabric gave way, leaving her neck bare.

To D'Artagnan's shock, one of the lovely white shoulders bore the fleur-de-lis: that permanent stamp imprinted by the executioner's hand!

"Great God!" cried D'Artagnan, releasing his hold of her dress, and remaining mute, motionless, and frozen.

Milady turned on him, no longer a furious woman, but like a wounded panther. She rushed towards her dressing table and drew out a dagger.

"Now you know my secret!" cried she. "You shall die." And she threw herself at D'Artagnan.

However, D'Artagnan designed to make his escape by the door leading to Kitty's apartment, and finally managed to flee. The young man ran at full speed across half of Paris, and did not stop till he reached Athos' door.

Athos was surprised to see his friend so early in the morning.

"Well," replied D'Artagnan, bending down to Athos' ear, and lowering his voice, "Milady is marked with a fleur-de-lis on her shoulder!"

"Ah!" cried the Musketeer.

"Come, now," said D'Artagnan, "are you sure that the other is dead?"

"The other?" said Athos, in such a stifled voice that D'Artagnan scarcely heard him.

Athos uttered a groan and let his head sink into his hands.

"She is fair," said he; "is she not?"

"Very."

"Clear, strangely brilliant blue eyes, with black eyelashes and eyebrows?"

"Yes."

"The fleur-de-lis is small, rose-coloured, and somewhat faint from the coat of paste applied to it?"

"Yes."

"But you said that she is an Englishwoman?"

"She is called Milady, but she may be French. Lord Winter is only her brother-in-law."

"I will see her, D'Artagnan. She was MY wife!"

CHAPTER 17

A Vision

At four o'clock, the four friends were all assembled in Athos' apartment, when Planchet entered, bringing two letters for D'Artagnan.

One was a little note neatly folded, with a pretty seal in green wax, on which there was the mark of a dove bearing a green branch.

The other was a large square letter, glittering

with the terrible arms of his Eminence, the Cardinal.

D'Artagnan seized the little letter and opened it eagerly. It said:

"On next Thursday, at seven o'clock in the evening, be on the road to Chaillot. Look carefully into the carriages that pass; but if you value your own life, or the life of those who love you, do not speak a word. Do not show that you recognise her, who exposes herself to everything for the sake of seeing you for an instant only."

There was no signature.

"That's a trap," said Athos. "Don't go, D'Artagnan."

"But, I think I recognise the writing," said D'Artagnan.

And then opening his second letter, he read:

"M. D'Artagnan, of the King's Guards, company Des Essarts, is expected at the palace of the Cardinal this evening at eight o'clock. Captain of the Guards."

"I will go to the second after attending the first," said D'Artagnan. "One is for seven o'clock and the other for eight; there will be time for both."

Just as it was quite twilight, a carriage appeared on the cited road, and almost instantly a woman put her head out at the window. She had two fingers placed on her mouth, either to instruct silence or to send D'Artagnan a kiss. D'Artagnan uttered a slight cry of joy. The woman was Madame Bonacieux.

The carriage pursued its way, still going at a full pace, till it dashed into Paris and disappeared.

D'Artagnan remained fixed to the spot, astonished, and not knowing what to think.

Half-past seven struck and he entered boldly at the front gate of the Cardinal's palace.

He entered the lobby and placed his letter in the hands of the officer on duty, who showed him into the waiting-room. After a few minutes, the man took him through the interior of the palace

and brought him before the Cardinal Richelieu.

The Cardinal looked at the young man for a moment. No one had a more probing eye than Cardinal Richelieu, and D'Artagnan felt this look run through his veins like a fever.

"Sit down there before me, Monsieur D'Artagnan," said his Eminence.

"You are brave, Monsieur D'Artagnan, and you are prudent, which is even better. But though you are young and have hardly entered on life, you have powerful enemies; if you do not take heed, they will destroy you!"

"Unfortunately, Monseigneur," replied the young man, "you are right. They can destroy me very easily, as they are strong and well supported, while I am alone."

"Yes, that's true. But alone as you are, you have already done much. Now, how about joining commission in my Guards, and a company after the campaign?"

"Ah, Monseigneur!"

"You accept it, do you not?"

"Monseigneur," replied D'Artagnan, with an embarrassed air.

"How? You refuse?" cried the Cardinal, with astonishment.

"I am in his Majesty's Guards, Monseigneur, and I have no reason to be dissatisfied," said D'Artagnan.

"That is to say, you refuse to serve me, sir," said the Cardinal in a tone of displeasure. "Remain free, then, and preserve your hatreds and your sympathies."

"Monseigneur…"

"Well, well!" said the Cardinal, "I am not angry with you, but I will give you a piece of advice: take good care of yourself, Monsieur D'Artagnan, for from this moment on I withdraw my hand from you."

"I will try to do so, Monseigneur," replied D'Artagnan, with a noble confidence.

And then, with a gesture, the Cardinal dismissed him.

D'Artagnan descended by the same staircase by which he had entered.

When he reached Athos' residence, Aramis and Porthos inquired about this strange interview; but D'Artagnan only told them that Richelieu had sent for him to suggest he enter his Guards with the rank of ensign, and that he had refused.

However, the young man sighed deeply, for a secret voice in his soul told him that great misfortunes were awaiting him.

CHAPTER 18

The Siege of Rochelle

The siege of the self-ruled La Rochelle was one of the great political events of Louis XIII's reign, and one of the Cardinal's great military enterprises.

The Cardinal wanted to have all of France under the Catholic rule and La Rochelle was the last town to be overpowered.

Rochelle and its port was the last gateway in the Kingdom of France open to the English, and by closing it against England, the Cardinal completed the work.

The King was to join the Cardinal at La Rochelle. But he was attacked by fever on the way. Although he was anxious to set out, his illness became more serious, and he was obliged to stop at Villeroi.

Now, whenever the King stopped, the Musketeers stopped. As a result, D'Artagnan, who was still in the Guards, was separated from his good friends Athos, Aramis and Porthos.

Everything had changed. The Duke of Buckingham and his English soldiers were closing in. But they couldn't succeed as the French army was already there.

At nine o'clock the next morning, the drums beat the salute. D'Artagnan passed along the front of the line. Then all the superior officers approached him to pay him their compliments.

D'Artagnan was so taken up with all this that he did not see Milady pointing him out to some sinister-looking, lowclass rogues.

The next day, D'Artagnan set out on a mission with four companions. He went near a small village where, the previous evening, he had been attacked by a few men. The men had fired gun shots at him.

While he was proceeding, D'Artagnan turned back and realised that the two soldiers who had accompanied him had disappeared. He thought that they had stayed behind from fear, and so he continued to advance with the other two.

On arriving at the angle of a ditch, one of the Guardsmen fell: a shot had passed through his breast. The other, who was safe and sound, kept on his way to camp.

But at that moment, two shots were fired. One hit the head of the already wounded guardsman, and the other flattened itself against a rock, after passing within two inches of D'Artagnan.

The young man turned quickly round, the idea of the two soldiers who had abandoned him came to his mind, and reminded him of the attacks of two evenings before. So he resolved this time to satisfy himself on this point, and fell on his comrade's body as though he were dead.

Instantly, two heads appeared, within thirty paces of him; they were the heads of his two missing soldiers!

Fortunately, deceived by D'Artagnan's trick, they had neglected to reload their guns. When they were within ten paces of him, D'Artagnan suddenly got up, and with one leap came upon them. One of the assassins took his gun by the barrel, and used it as he would use a club. He aimed a terrible blow at D'Artagnan. D'Artagnan escaped it by springing on one side; and then he threw himself on the other soldier, attacking him with his sword.

The struggle did not last long. D'Artagnan immediately placed the point of the weapon at the soldier's throat.

"Villain," cried D'Artagnan, "speak quickly! Who employed you to assassinate me?"

"A woman whom I don't know, but who is called Milady," cried the terrified soldier.

"But if you don't know this woman, how do you know her name?" asked D'Artagnan.

"My comrade knew her and called her so, he has a letter from that person even now in his pocket, which must be of great importance to you."

D'Artagnan searched and found a letter which said that Madame Bonacieux was now in safety in the convent.

He returned to the camp with his wounded comrade.

D'Artagnan felt very uneasy, as he had not heard from his friends for a long time.

But one morning early in November he got a letter, dated from Villeroi:

"Monsieur   D'Artagnan,—MM.   Athos, Porthos, and Aramis are confined for some days in the castle of our provost. On their request, I am sending bottles of my Anjou wine which they would like you to enjoy. Your obedient servant, Godeau, Steward of the Musketeers."

"That's good!" cried D'Artagnan. "They think of me in their pleasures, as I think of them in my troubles. Well, I will certainly drink to their health with all my heart, but I will not drink alone."

And D'Artagnan went to two guardsmen with whom he had had become friends. They decided to have a feast and enjoy the wine the very next day.

The next day, as the guests were on the point of touching the first glass of wine to their lips, they suddenly heard cannon roar and heard the cries of "Hurrah for the King! Hurrah for the Cardinal!" resounding on every side. The King had just arrived with his entire household and a reinforcement of ten thousand troops. His Musketeers rode in front of him and behind him. As soon as the reception ceremony was over, the four friends were soon in one another's arms. When they saw the table laid with the feast and the wine in the glasses, all of them were very happy. D' Artagnan offered the wine to them, telling them that it was the same wine they had sent him.

"We sent you wine?" cried all three together.

"Yes; you know what I mean—the wine from the slopes of Anjou."

"Did you send this wine, Aramis?" said Athos.

"No; and you, Porthos?" said Aramis.

"No; and you, Athos?" said Porthos.

"No!"

"Well, but if it was not you, it was your steward," said D'Artagnan.

"Our steward!"

"Here is his letter," said D'Artagnan, and he showed them the letter.

"That is not his writing!" said Athos; "I know it."

"It is a forged letter," said Porthos.

D'Artagnan rushed inside. There, he saw one of the Musketeers he had invited to dine with, lying dead on the floor!

D'Artagnan immediately knew it was another of Milady's schemes to kill him.

CHAPTER 19

The Tavern of the Red Dovecot

One evening, a few days later, Athos, Porthos and Aramis were returning on horse back to their camp, when they heard the trampling of horses approaching them. All three instantly halted, closed in, and waited, occupying the middle of the road. Just as the moon came out from behind a cloud, they saw two horsemen appear at a turn in the road. The men stopped when they saw the three Musketeers.

Athos rode up a few paces in advance of the others and cried in a firm voice, "Who goes there?"

"You tell us who you are?" replied one of the two horsemen.

"That is not an answer," replied Athos. "Answer, or else we charge."

"Your name?" insisted the horseman, letting his cloak fall, and leaving his face uncovered.

"The Cardinal!" cried the astonished Musketeer.

"Your name?" cried his Eminence yet again.

"Athos," said the Musketeer.

The Cardinal made a sign to his attendant, who drew near to him.

"These three Musketeers shall follow us," said he in an undertone. "I do not wish it to be known that I left the camp; and by following us we shall be certain they will tell no one."

The three Musketeers bowed to the necks of their horses and fell behind his Eminence, who again enveloped his face in his cloak and started up his horse.

They soon reached a silent, solitary tavern. The landlord knew beforehand who was coming to his tavern, and had sent intruders away.

At ten paces from the door, the Cardinal made a sign to his attendant and the three Musketeers to halt. Then he alighted; the three Musketeers followed his example. The Cardinal threw the bridle of his horse to his attendant and the three Musketeers fastened their horses to the shutters.

The landlord stood at the door; for him, the Cardinal was only an officer coming to visit a lady.

"Do you have a room on the ground floor with a good fire where these gentlemen can wait?" the Cardinal asked.

"I have one, sir," said he.

And while the three Musketeers were shown

to a ground-floor room, the Cardinal, without asking further information, mounted the staircase like a man who knew his way.

'Now who was that someone the Cardinal was to meet?' The three Musketeers put this question to each other.

Athos walked about in thoughtful mood. While walking, he kept passing and re-passing by the stove-pipe, broken in half, the other end of which went into the upper chamber. Every time he passed, he heard a murmur of words. This attracted his attention. Athos went close to it, beckoned to his friends to be silent, and placed his ear against the lower opening.

"...listen, Milady," came the Cardinal's voice; "the affair is important. Sit down and let us talk."

"Milady!" murmured Athos.

"I am listening to your Eminence with the greatest attention," replied a woman's voice that shocked the Musketeer.

The Cardinal instructed her to leave for

England immediately, and informed her that two men whom she would find while going out of the inn would escort her.

A brief silence followed this, and then the Cardinal spoke again.

"You will go to London," continued the Cardinal; "When you reach London you will inquire about Buckingham and you will present yourself frankly and loyally as a negotiator. You will go to Buckingham on my behalf, and you will tell him I am aware of all his plans and at the first step he takes, I will ruin the Queen."

"Will he believe that your Eminence is in a position to carry out the threat you make?" said Milady.

"I believe he knows that," said the Cardinal, "Here are some papers - proof of what I said."

"Is that all, Monseigneur?"

"Well," said the Cardinal, "that is it."

"And now," said Milady, "that I have received your Eminence's instructions regarding your enemies, will Monseigneur permit me to say a few words of mine?"

"What is it?" asked the Cardinal.

"In the first place, there is a woman named Bonacieux."

"She is in a convent."

"I don't know which one; the secret has been well kept."

"But I will know!"

"And will your Eminence tell me in which convent this woman is?"

"I see nothing improper in that," said the Cardinal.

"Well, now I have an enemy whom I dread much more than this little Madame Bonacieux."

"Who is that?"

"Her lover."

"What is his name?"

"D'Artagnan."

"He is a bold fellow," said the Cardinal. "I must have proof of his connection with Buckingham."

"Proof!" cried Milady, "I will find you plenty."

"Well, then, it is the simplest thing in the world. Get me your proof, and I will send him to the Bastille."

"Monseigneur," replied Milady, "a fair exchange - life for life, man for man; give me one, I will give you the other."

"Well then give me a paper, a pen, and some ink," said the Cardinal.

"Here they are, monseigneur."

Athos and his friends heard it all.

"I must be gone," Athos told them.

"And what should we say if the Cardinal asks for you?" said Porthos with surprise.

"Tell him that I have gone as a scout, to check the safety of the road."

Athos went out without anybody being suspicious about his leaving and Porthos and Aramis resumed their places by the stove-pipe.

The Cardinal came back and asked the Musketeers to join him for their return to the

camp. When he asked about Athos, he was told that he had left to scout the road. The soldiers at the gate also confirmed the same, and so they left.

For a hundred paces, Athos maintained the speed with which he started, but once out of sight, he turned his horse to the right, and at a gallop returned to the tavern, which was opened to him without hesitation.

The landlord recognised him.

"My officer," said Athos "has forgotten to give a piece of very important information to the lady."

"Go up," said the host; "she is still in her room."

He went straight into the chamber and closed the door behind him.

Milady heard the noise of the door bolt and turned around.

She was startled.

"Who are you, and what do you want?" cried she.

"There now!" murmured Athos; "it is certainly the same woman!"

And dropping his cloak and raising his hat, towards Milady.

"Do you know me, Madame?" said Athos.

Milady took one step forward, and then grew pale.

"The Comte de la Fère!" she murmured.

"Yes, I am the Comte de la Fère," said Athos.

"You believed me to be dead, did you not, as I believed you to be? All these years the name of Athos had concealed the Comte de la Fère, just as the name Milady Clarik concealed Anne de Breuil."

"But," said Milady, in a hollow, faint voice, "what brings you back to me? And what do you want with me?"

"I wish to tell you that though I was invisible to your eyes, I have not lost sight of you. I can relate to you, day by day, your actions from the day of your entry to the service of the Cardinal, to this evening."

"You must be Satan!" cried she.

"Perhaps, but listen carefully to what I say. Do not touch with the tip of your finger a single hair of D'Artagnan or I swear to you that you shall die. He is a faithful friend whom I love and will defend."

Then Athos raised his pistol and put it to Milady's forehead. "Madame," he said, "give me the paper the Cardinal signed, right now!"

Milady pulled out a paper, and held it towards Athos.

"Take it," said she, "curse on you!"

Athos took the paper and read:

"August 5, 1628.

By my order, and for the good of the State, the bearer of this paper has done what he has done upon my orders.

Richelieu."

Athos left the chamber without once looking behind him, leaped lightly into his saddle, and set out at full gallop. Only, instead of following the road, he galloped across the fields, urging his horse to the utmost, and stopping occasionally to listen.

He arrived just in time to meet the Cardinal and his friends approaching the camp.

CHAPTER 20

A Family Affair

The four friends decided to go to the Fortress of Saint-Gervais to have a talk.

The fortress was occupied only by a dozen dead bodies, French and Rochellais.

The four friends sat down at the fortress, and Grimaud laid out the breakfast, while Planchet removed the dead bodies.

After a while, Grimaud announced that

breakfast was ready.

"And now, let's eat!," said Athos.

"But what is the secret?" said D'Artagnan.

"The secret is," said Athos, "that I saw Milady last night."

"And where?" demanded D'Artagnan.

"About two leagues from here, at the tavern of the Red Dovecot." And Athos described the events that had taken place at the tavern.

"Do you know," said Porthos, "that to twist Milady's neck would not be a sin?"

"I say I am entirely of Porthos' opinion," replied Aramis.

"And I too," said D'Artagnan.

"I have an idea," said D'Artagnan.

"What is it?" cried the Musketeers.

Athos looked at his watch.

"Gentlemen," said he, "let's hear out D'Artagnan."

"Well, I will go to England again; I will go and find Buckingham," said D'Artagnan.

"You shall not do that, D'Artagnan, as we are at war now," said Athos coolly.

"This Milady—this woman—this creature—this demon has a brother-inlaw, as I think you have told me, D'Artagnan?"

"Yes, I know him very well; and I also believe that he does not have a very warm affection for his sister-in-law."

"What is her brother-in-law's name?"

"Lord Winter."

"Well, he's just the man we want," said Athos. "We must warn him. We will send him a message that his sister- in-law is on the point of assassinating some one and we will beg of him not to lose sight of her."

And they decided to send their lackey to Lord Winter.

The next day, they went for breakfast at M. de Tréville's. D'Artagnan, who was ranked a Musketeer by the Cardinal the night before, was already in his uniform. He would have been the happiest person on earth if he had not constantly seen Milady, like a dark cloud, on the horizon.

In the evening, at the appointed hour, the four friends met. They wrote a note to Milady's brother-in-law, asking him to be careful as there was a plot being woven to murder him, and handed it over to Planchet.

Planchet mounted on an excellent horse and set off at a gallop.

On the sixteenth day, Planchet came back and slipped a note into D'Artagnan's hand, which the four friends read together. The note just said:

"Be easy. Thanks."

In the meantime, Milady, drunk with rage, continued her voyage, and reached London the day Planchet returned to France.

At the port, a young officer from the navy received her, and to Milady's surprise asked her to come with him. Milady, though suspicious of the young man, followed him into a carriage without any questions.

The officer saw that the baggage was fastened carefully behind the carriage; then he took his place beside Milady, and shut the door.

Instantly, without any order being given, or place of destination being indicated, the coachman set off at a gallop, and plunged into the streets of the town. After an hour, the carriage stopped and they alighted in front of a castle. Milady entered the place, and the men followed with her baggage.

After a while, Milady could hold out no longer and she broke the silence.

"In the name of Heaven, sir," cried she, "what is the meaning of all this?"

"Madame, I was instructed to receive you at the port and bring you here."

At that moment, the door opened and a man appeared on the threshold.

To her amazement, Milady recognised the man as her brother-in-law, Lord Winter.

Lord Winter thanked the officer and asked him to leave.

"So, let us talk, brother," said Milady.

But Lord Winter was by now aware of all her plans. He did not wish to talk to her anymore and left hastily. She was left in the custody of Officer Felton and another officer.

To her horror, Milady realised that she had been made a prisoner.

That night, before she went to bed, Milady analysed the two officers who were on guard, and realised that Felton was the more vulnerable of the two.

"Weak or strong," thought Milady, "that man has a spark of pity in his soul. He is young and ingenious, and seems virtuous; these are the means of destroying him."

And Milady went to bed, and fell asleep with a smile on her lips.

The next morning, when Felton came to see her, he found Milady on her knees saying her prayers and crying. Felton found a feeling of sympathy growing in him, and went up to her.

"Sir," cried Milady, "be kind, listen to my prayer."

And she narrated a false story about her life to Felton. She told him how she had always been misused by the Duke of Buckingham.

Felton was smitten by Milady's beauty and shaken by her tale of woe.

Milady further narrated to him a fictitious story about how Buckingham maltreated and abused her, and when she resisted him, he branded her with the fleur-de-lis. When Felton saw the dreadful mark, he was so overcome with passion and fury that he vowed to do anything for her.

When Milady saw that Felton was ready to avenge her, she smiled to herself. She knew that Felton was her only hope, her only means of safety.

The next morning, Milady sent away the woman who attended her, under the pretence of not having slept during the night and wanting rest. She waited for Felton all day but Felton didn't appear.

At night, she suddenly heard a tap at her window.

She ran to the window and opened it.

"Felton!" cried she, "I am saved!"

"Yes," said Felton, "but be silent, be silent!"

Milady shut the window, extinguished the lamp, and went to lie down on the bed.

At the end of an hour, Felton tapped again.

Milady sprang out of bed, opened the window and climbed on a chair.

Felton had removed two bars making an opening large enough for a man to pass through, thus enabling Milady to slip easily out of it. Felton then helped Milady climb down a rope ladder.

They safely reached the port where Felton had hired a boat for her.

"Buckingham sets sail tomorrow for Rochelle!" Felton informed Milady.

"He must not sail!" cried Milady.

"Do not worry!" replied Felton; "he will not sail."

Then he told Milady that he would get down to Portsmouth in order to take his revenge on Buckingham before Buckingham left for France.

Milady was content with this answer. She knew that Felton would go to any extent to stop the Duke of Buckingham. Then, Felton climbed up the ladder of the ship first, and helped Milady up on the deck.

"Captain," said Felton, "this is the lady of whom I spoke, and whom you must convey safe and sound to France."

Then, Milady and Felton decided that she should wait in the ship for Felton till ten o'clock. If he did not return by then, she was to sail without him.

In that case, and supposing he was not captured, Felton would meet her in France, at the convent of the Carmelites at Béthune.

CHAPTER 21

What took place at Portsmouth, August 23, 1628

Felton left Milady and entered Portsmouth at about eight o'clock in the morning. The whole population was on foot, and drums were beating in the streets and in the port. The troops, about to go on board, were marching towards the sea. The Duke of Buckingham was to set sail for France with all his troops.

Felton arrived at the palace of the Duke, covered with dust and streaming with perspiration. He was in a naval officer's uniform. His face was purple with excitement. The guard was about to keep him away, but Felton called to the officer of the post, and drawing a letter from his pocket, he said, "An urgent message from Lord Winter."

At the name of Lord Winter, who was known to be one of his Grace's most intimate friends, the officer gave orders to let Felton pass.

Felton darted into the palace.

As he was entering the hall, he saw another man also enter the hall. He too was covered with dust and out of breath. Felton and the other man addressed Patrick, the Duke's confidential valet at the same time. Felton named Lord Winter, the stranger gave no name, and each insisted on seeing the Duke first.

Patrick led Felton first as he knew the Duke was a friend of Lord Winter. Felton entered with a knife in his hand. Buckingham, who was in his room getting ready for the sail, looked at Felton and asked, "Why didn't the baron come himself? I expected him this morning."

"He desired me to tell your Grace," replied Felton, "that he very much regretted not having that honour, but that he was prevented by the guard he is obliged to keep at the castle."

"Yes, I know that," said Buckingham; "he has a prisoner."

"It is of that prisoner that I wish to speak to your Grace," replied Felton.

"Well, then, speak!"

"What I have to say, can only be heard by yourself, my Lord!"

"Leave us, Patrick," said Buckingham; "but remain close by. I shall call you presently."

Patrick went out.

"We are alone, sir," said Buckingham. "Speak!"

"My Lord," said Felton, "I would request you not to sign the order of embarkation of Milady de

Winter."

On hearing this, Buckingham was quite shocked and an argument broke out between them. Gradually, the argument became fierce and Buckingham called for Patrick, Felton accused the Duke of dishonouring Milady and screamed that he would avenge her. At that moment, Patrick, who had heard his master's calls, rushed into the room. He also carried a letter in his hand.

"A letter from France, my Lord," said he.

"From France!" exclaimed Buckingham, forgetting everything. Felton took advantage of this moment, and with one leap, he was upon the Duke and plunged the knife into his side up to the handle.

"Ah, traitor," cried Buckingham, "you have killed me!"

"Murder!" screamed Patrick.

Felton cast his eyes around for means of escape, and seeing the door free, he rushed into the next chamber and then rushed towards the staircase. But upon the first step, he met Lord Winter. He, seeing Felton pale and both his hands stained with blood, seized him by the throat, crying, "I knew it! I guessed it! But unfortunately I was late by a minute!"

Then, he handed him over to the Guards, who by then had surrounded them. When Milady saw that Felton didn't come as decided earlier, she set sail for France at the stroke of eight.

CHAPTER 22

Another Act of Murder

Milady passed through the cruisers of both nations, and reached France without any accident. There, she posted a letter to the Cardinal that read:

"Monseigneur, be reassured: his Grace the Duke of Buckingham will not set out for France."

"Lady de –."

"P.S.—According to your Eminence's wish, I am going to the convent at Béthune, where I will await your orders."

Meanwhile, D'Artagnan and his friends were also on their way to the convent in Béthune.

In fact, that same evening Milady had begun her journey. At night, she stopped and slept at an inn. At five o'clock the next morning, she was on her way again, and three hours later, she entered Béthune.

She inquired for the Carmelite convent, and went there immediately.

The Mother Superior of the convent met her at the door. Milady told her that she had come to see a lady who was sent by the Queen and showed her the Cardinal's order. Milady was given a room and breakfast, and then, growing very impatient, she asked the Mother Superior, "And when can I see the young lady, for whom I have come so far?"

"Why, this evening," said the nun; "today even.

But you have been travelling these four days, as you told me yourself. You must rest for some time and then I will send her to meet you."

In the evening, the Mother Superior brought Madame Bonacieux to her room and introduced them to each other. Then she left the two young women alone to talk. As soon as the Mother Superior had left, Milady said, "I know you, you are Madame Bonacieux."

The young woman drew back in surprise and terror.

"Oh, do not deny it! Answer!" continued Milady.

"Well, yes, Madame!" said the novice.

Milady's face was lit with such a savage joy that in any other circumstances Madame Bonacieux would have fled in terror.

"Can you not understand that M. D'Artagnan, who is my friend, has told me about you?" said Milady.

"Indeed!"

"Ah, dear Constance, I have found you, then; I see you at last!"

And Milady stretched out her arms to Madame Bonacieux, who, convinced by what she had just said, saw nothing in this woman but a sincere and devoted friend.

Milady arose and went to the door, opened it, looked down the corridor, and then returned and seated herself near Madame Bonacieux.

"Is D'Artagnan coming?"

"D'Artagnan and his friends are detained at the siege of Rochelle."

Milady suggested that they should ride back to Paris and asked her to have some food and wine before they started on the journey.

Madame Bonacieux ate a few mouthfuls mechanically, and just as she was touching the glass to her lips, she heard the neighing of horses.

They couldn't see anybody, but only heard the galloping constantly draw nearer.

Madame Bonacieux remained standing, mute,

pale, and motionless.

Suddenly, at a turn in the road, Milady saw the glitter of laced hats and the waving plumes; she counted two, then five, then eight horsemen.

In the first horseman, she recognised D'Artagnan. Milady uttered a stifled groan.

"O Heavens, Heavens!" cried Madame Bonacieux, "What is it? What is it?"

"It is the Cardinal's Guards—we should not waste a second!" cried Milady.

"Let us run from here!"

"Yes, yes, let us run away!" repeated Madame Bonacieux.

They heard the horsemen riding under the windows.

"Come on, then! Do come on!" cried Milady.

Madame Bonacieux tried to walk, took two steps, and sank to her knees.

Milady tried to lift her up and carry her, but could not succeed.

All at once, Milady stopped and ran to the table, opened her ring and poured into Madame Bonacieux's glass the contents of a ring.

Then taking the glass with a firm hand, she said, "Drink this wine, it will give you strength— drink!"

With these words, she put the glass to the lips of the young woman, who drank mechanically.

Immediately, Milady rushed out of the room.

All at once, Constance heard D'Artagnan's voice and uttered a loud cry of joy.

"D'Artagnan! D'Artagnan!" cried she, "Is it you? This way! This way!"

"Constance! Constance!" cried the young man, "Where are you? My God!"

At the same moment, the door of the cell yielded to a blow, and opened.

Several men rushed into the room.

Meanwhile, Madame Bonacieux had sunk into an armchair, unable to move.

"O D'Artagnan! My beloved D'Artagnan! You

have come, then, at last. You have not deceived
me! It is indeed you!"

"Yes, yes, Constance!"

"Help, friends, help! Her hands are like ice!"
cried D'Artagnan. "She is ill! Great God, she is
becoming unconscious!"

"Madame," said Athos—"Madame, in
Heaven's name, whose empty glass is this?"

"Mine, sir," said the young woman, in a dying

"...ut who poured out for you the wine that ... this glass?"

"...e Countess Winter," said Madame ...eux, and those were her last words.

The four friends uttered one and the same cry, but the cry of Athos dominated over all the rest. D'Artagnan, who was heartbroken, held the dead body of Madame Bonacieux and burst into violent sobs.

Athos rose, walked up to his friend with a slow and solemn step, and with his noble and persuasive voice, he said, "Friend, be a man! Women weep for the dead; men avenge them!"

And as affectionately as a father, he drew away his friend.

All five, followed by their lackeys leading their horses, made their way to the town of Béthune.

"But," D'Artagnan asked Athos as they were on their way, "are we not going to follow that woman?"

"No this vengeance belongs to me," said Athos. "I owe that at least to my wife. I take charge of everything. Do not worry."

D'Artagnan had such trust in his friend's word that he bowed his head, and entered the inn without giving a reply.

Porthos and Aramis looked at each other, not at all understanding Athos' confidence.

Athos was the last to retire to his room that night. He was possessed by a single thought— that of the promise he had made, and of the responsibility he had assumed.

He sent Planchet, Grimaud, Bazin, and Mousqueton in search of Milady and asked to report the next day at eleven o'clock. If they found Milady, three were to remain on guard; the fourth was to return to Béthune, to inform Athos.

When these arrangements were made, the lackeys retired.

Planchet came back the next day and informed him where Milady was staying.

At eight o'clock in the evening Athos notified Lord Winter, (who had joined them after following Milady to Paris) and his other friends to prepare for the expedition. In an instant, all five were ready. Athos was the last to come down, and found D'Artagnan already on horseback and impatient.

"Patience!" cried Athos. "One of us is still lacking."

The four gentlemen looked round them in astonishment, as they wondered who this some one lacking could be.

"Wait for me," cried Athos. "I will be back."

And he set off at a gallop.

In a quarter of an hour he returned, accompanied by a tall masked man enveloped in a large red cloak.

Lord Winter and the three Musketeers looked at one another inquiringly, but Athos didn't give them any explanation.

At nine o'clock, guided by Planchet, they set out.

CHAPTER 23

The Judgment

In a while, they reached the house where Milady was. Athos went up to a window to peep in. At this moment, a horse neighed. This made Milady raise her head and she saw Athos' pale face close to the window. She screamed in terror.

Athos pushed the window with his knee, and jumped into the room.

Milady ran to the door to escape but D'Artagnan stood on the threshold.

She drew back, uttering a cry.

"Come in, gentlemen," said Athos.

D'Artagnan, Porthos, Aramis, Lord Winter, and the man in the red cloak, all entered the room.

The four lackeys guarded the door and the window.

"What do you want?" screamed Milady.

"We intend to judge you according to your crimes," said Athos. "You shall be free to defend yourself. Justify yourself if you can. Monsieur D'Artagnan, it is for you to accuse her first."

D'Artagnan stepped forward.

"I accuse this woman of poisoning Constance Bonacieux, who died yesterday evening," said D'Artagnan. "And I accuse this woman of having tried to poison me by wine which she sent me from Villeroi, with a forged letter."

"We bear witness to this," said Porthos and

Aramis, in the same voice.

"It is your turn, My Lord," said Athos.

"Before God and before men," said Lord Winter, "I accuse this woman of having caused the assassination of the Duke of Buckingham."

And Lord Winter went to stand by D'Artagnan's side, leaving his place free for another accuser.

Milady buried her face in her two hands.

"It is my turn," said Athos, "I married this woman when she was a young girl. One day I discovered that this woman was branded – this woman was marked with a fleur-de-lis on her left shoulder."

"Oh," said Milady, "I challenge you to find the court which pronounced that infamous sentence upon me. I challenge you to find him who executed it."

"Silence!" said a voice. "It is for me to reply to that!"

And the man in the red cloak came forward in his turn.

"Who is this man? Who is this man?" cried Milady.

All eyes were fixed on this man.

The unknown took off his mask. Milady, for some time, examined with increasing terror his pale face. Then all at once she cried in a hoarse voice,

"Oh no, no! It is not he! The executioner! The executioner of Lille!"

Everyone drew back in surprise, and the man in the red cloak remained standing alone in the middle of the room.

"Oh, forgive me, pardon, pardon me!" cried the wretched woman, falling on her knees.

The stranger spoke up now:

"This young woman was a nun. A young priest, of a simple and believing heart, was the chaplain of that convent. She enticed this man into her love and made him run away with her after stealing things from the church.

However, both were caught and sent to jail.

In jail, this woman managed to charm the jailor's son and escape. Meanwhile, the young priest was condemned to ten years in chains, and was branded. I was the executioner of the city of Lille, and was obliged to brand the guilty man. That man was my brother!"

"I then swore that this woman, who had ruined him, should share at least his punishment. I found her and I imprinted the same disgraceful mark on her that I had imprinted on my poor brother. My brother then escaped from jail. I was accused of helping him and was jailed for it. In the meantime, my brother had rejoined this woman. They fled together into Berry, and there he obtained a little curacy. This woman called herself his sister."

"The lord of the estate on which the curate's church was situated fell in love with her and he offered to marry her. Then this woman left him whom she had ruined, and became the Comtesse de la Fère —"

All eyes were turned towards Athos, whose

real name was this.

"Then," resumed the other, "sad and depressed, my poor brother returned to Lille, and killed himself. But with his return my innocence was established, and I was freed."

"That is the crime of which I accuse her. That is the cause of her being branded."

"Monsieur D'Artagnan, Milord de Winter, M. Porthos and M. Aramis, what penalty do you demand against this woman?" asked Athos.

"The penalty of death," replied all of them.

Athos stretched out his hand towards her.

"Charlotte Backson, Comtesse de la Fére, Milady de Winter," said he, "your crimes have exhausted men on earth and God in heaven. If you know any prayer, say it; as we sentence you to death."

Milady knew she was doomed now. She did not even attempt to make any resistance, and went out of the cottage.

Lord Winter, D'Artagnan, Athos, Porthos, and

Aramis followed her. The lackeys followed their masters.

It was almost midnight. Two of the lackeys dragged Milady along, each taking one of her arms. The executioner walked behind them, and Lord Winter, D'Artagnan, Porthos, and Aramis walked behind the executioner.

When they reached the banks of the river Lys, the executioner approached Milady and bound her hands and her feet.

Athos took a step towards Milady.

"I pardon you," said he, "for the ill you have done to me."

They took her in a boat to the other end of the shore and the executioner raised the sword and brought it down on her neck. That was the end of Milady.

In the middle of the stream, the executioner stopped the boat, and held his burden over the water.

"Let the justice of God be done!" cried he, in a loud voice and let the body drop into the depths of the waters.

Three days later, the four Musketeers were in Paris again, and the very same evening they went to pay their customary visit to M. de Trèville.

CHAPTER 24

Conclusion

On the sixth of the following month, the King returned to La Rochelle with all his army and his Musketeers by his side. The King was overjoyed to hear that his enemy, the Duke of Buckingham was dead.

The Queen, on the other hand was deep in despair. She was not ready to believe the news of the death of her beloved.

One day, when the king had stopped to fly the magpie (a pastime for which he had a great fondness), the four friends, instead of taking part in the sport, went to a tavern. A man, riding full speed from La Rochelle, pulled up at the door to have some wine, and glanced into the room where the four Musketeers were sitting at a table.

"Hello, Monsieur D'Artagnan!" said he, as he noticed D'Artagnan.

D'Artagnan raised his head and uttered a cry of suprise. It was the stranger of Meung.

D'Artagnan drew his sword and sprang towards the door.

The stranger then leaped from his horse and came forward to meet him.

"Ah, sir!" said D'Artagnan, "I meet you, at last! This time you shall not escape me!"

"It is not my intention to either. I arrest you in the name of the King. I tell you that you must surrender your sword to me and follow me."

"But who are you?" demanded D'Artagnan, lowering the point of his sword.

"I am the Chevalier de Rochefort," answered the stranger, "Cardinal Richelieu's officer, and I have orders to take you to his Eminence."

So, the man, whom D'Artagnan had searched for all this time, was actually the Cardinal's right hand man!

"We are returning to La Rochelle and D'Artagnan will report to the Cardinal," said Athos.

"But I must place him in the hands of Guards who will take him to camp," said Rochefort.

"We will serve as his Guards, sir, take my word," added Athos. "M. D'Artagnan shall not leave us."

Rochefort then decided to go back to Rochelle with his prisoner and the Musketeers.

When the Cardinal returned from the King's court, he found D'Artagnan standing before the house without his sword, and the three Musketeers armed. The Cardinal made a sign for D'Artagnan to follow him.

D'Artagnan obeyed.

"We shall wait for you, D'Artagnan," said Athos, loud enough for the Cardinal to hear him.

His Eminence went to the room which served him as a study, and made a sign to Rochefort to bring in the young Musketeer.

Rochefort ushered D'Artagnan in and left him with the Cardinal.

"Sir," said the Cardinal, "you have been arrested by my orders."

"So I have been told, monseigneur."

"You are charged with having corresponded with the enemies of the Kingdom."

"And who charges me with this, monseigneur?" said D'Artagnan. "A lady who herself has committed endless crimes!"

D'Artagnan then related the poisoning of Madame Bonacieux at the Carmelite convent of Béthune, the trial in the lonely house, and the execution on the banks of the Lys.

"I also have my pardon signed by you for anything I have done," said he.

"Your pardon?" said Richelieu, surprised. "By me? You are mad, sir!"

"Monseigneur will doubtless recognise his own writing."

And D'Artagnan presented to the Cardinal the precious paper which Athos had forcefully taken from Milady, and which he had given to D'Artagnan to serve him as a safeguard.

His Eminence took the paper and read in a slow voice, dwelling on every syllable:

"August 5, 1628.

By my order, and for the good of the State, the bearer of this paper has done what he has done upon my orders. Richelieu."

Richelieu slowly tore the paper which D'Artagnan had handed over without thinking twice.

"I am lost!" said D'Artagnan to himself.

The Cardinal then went to the table, and without sitting down, wrote a few lines on a paper, two-thirds of which was already filled out, and affixed his seal to it.

"Here, sir," said the Cardinal to the young man.

D'Artagnan took the paper hesitatingly, and thought, "This is my punishment, now I will be sent to the Bastille."

Then slowly, as he read the letter, he jumped with joy.

It was a lieutenant's commission in the Musketeers and it was not addressed to anyone. The Cardinal explained that it was for D'Artagnan to fill it out.

D'Artagnan fell at the Cardinal's feet.

"Monseigneur," said he, "my life is yours! But I do not deserve this favour which you confer on me. I have three friends who are more meritorious and more worthy –"

"You are an honest fellow, D'Artagnan,"

interrupted the Cardinal. "Do whatever you want with it."

"I shall never forget it," replied D'Artagnan. "Your Eminence may be certain of that."

He bowed to his Eminence, left the room, and met his friends who were waiting impatiently for him.

"Here I am, friends," replied D'Artagnan— "not only free, but in favour."

"Will you tell us about it?"

He told them what had taken place between the Cardinal and himself, and drawing the paper from his pocket, said "Here, my dear Athos; the commission naturally belongs to you."

Athos smiled his sweet, fascinating smile.

"My friend," said he, "Keep it; it is yours. It has cost you enough."

D'Artagnan then offered it to his other two friends, who answered him similarly.

Then Athos took a pen, wrote D'Artagnan's name on the commission, and returned it to him, saying, "Here, D'Artagnan, the lieutenancy is now yours."

"I shall then no longer have any friends," said the young man from Gascon with tears in his eyes. D'Artagnan was both happy and sad to leave his friends and join the Cardinal's commission.

Then Athos, Porthos and Aramis reassured him that they would always remain friends. And thus, D'Artagnan of Gascony became an officer in the commission.

THE END